GIANT TALES
3-MINUTE STORIES

FROM THE
MISTY SWAMP

GIANT TALES

FROM THE
MISTY SWAMP

Introduction by
PROFESSOR K.R. LIMN

Professor Limn Books
Charlotte, North Carolina

For information, please write to: H. M. Schuldt
heathermarieschuldt.blogspot.com

Cover Illustrations are from the public domain
Cover Art © 2013 Northlake Art Studio

First published in 2013 by Professor Limn Books LLC
ISBN 9780988578425

Second Edition, January 2014

To Mrs. Mapes,
my fourth grade English teacher
who started me on my journey as a writer

Preface

Most of the 3-minute tales
in this book really did not happen.
Each author created new characters
who encounter a crisis
set in a fictitious world.
Giant Tales From the Misty Swamp
is a work of fiction.
I have a love for reading fiction,
whether long or short,
and I find myself baking up
new stories all day long
wherever I might be.
With a sense of wonder,
I am delighted to see
how authors in this book
took a good look at life,
and with great creativity,
demonstrated how easily
life can be turned upside down.
Not only do the stories come alive,
but the authors themselves
jump right off the page.
Take a walk into the misty swamp,
experience all new stories,
and find out how some lives
have been changed forever.

PROFESSOR K.R. LIMN

PART ONE

Contents

CHAPTER ONE

MISTY SWAMP

CHAPTER TWO

CLIMATE CHANGE

CHAPTER THREE

CARNIVAL

CHAPTER FOUR

MASKS

AFTERWORD

Arlene Lagos
Douglas G. Clarke
Laura Stafford
Kristen Strassel
Jot Russell
Richard Bunning
Alli Vaughan
Harry Alexiou
Oliver Dolan
H.M. Schuldt
Randy Dutton
Gail Harkins
Sylvia Stein
Lynette White
Janet Bond
Colleen Sayre
Scott Amis
Andy Lake
Jenise Erikson
Mike Boggia

INTRODUCTION

Have you ever found yourself wanting to explore a new world of quiet maple trees or would you rather go find a lively carnival? Here in this book, you will find trees and carnivals in a swamp— a mysterious foggy misty swamp. You'll find stories full of suspense, of course, because visibility has become limited and danger could be several feet ahead. Adventure is found in a thick drizzly wooded swamp, a place where amphibians are about to jump right off the page. Take a look at how *climate change* can affect people in ways you've never seen before. Feel the clock ticking when characters set out to find one other. Most certainly, this is a wonderfully crafted book.

Come see how twenty authors did a remarkable job using the themes of disguises, a race against time, and a search for something lost. I am very pleased to present book two, *Giant Tales From the Misty Swamp*, the second of three Giant Tales anthologies from 2013. I invite you sit back, relax, and get ready to discover the *misty swamp*.

PROFESSOR K.R. LIMN

CHAPTER 1

MISTY SWAMP

WAKING

by
Arlene Lagos

It feels like I've been running for hours. Surprisingly my feet don't hurt even though they're covered in cuts and bruises. Stopping to check my left side where I hit the road after jumping from the moving vehicle, I see a large gash and some dried blood. Shock must be setting in because I feel nothing at all. Sliding down the side of a large maple tree beside a muddy swamp, I hold my head in my hands trying to put the pieces back together.

We had been arguing in the car. Jake was driving, swerving, and drunk. He struck me in the jaw. I was rolling down a hill and into the woods. Jake wasn't perfect. He drank a lot. And sometimes he got loud, and sometimes I got hit. I knew when to keep my mouth shut. But this time was different. This time he seemed unable to control himself.

Staring into the swamp, I see something move and distance myself less I be eaten. The wind gusts up a cyclone of leaves that surround me. Frightened, I walk fast in the opposite direction. A few minutes later I find myself back at the swamp.

"How on earth?"

"You can't leave," says a voice.

Spinning around I find a young man in his teens standing in front of me. His face is pale and lifeless. Darting as fast as I can in the other direction, I try to outrun him, just to find him standing in front of me.

"How did you do that?" I gasp.

"I'm dead. I died here a few years ago. They still haven't found my body, so they probably won't find yours either."

He points to a small area near the edge of the swamp where I see my hand jutting out of the leaves. My favorite bracelet is dangling off the end of it.

"I don't..."

"You don't remember, but I saw the whole thing. That man beat you in the side of the head with a rock and buried you in the ground just a few inches from me. That's why you can't leave. You're soul is tied to your body," he explains.

"Jake...killed me?"

"Jake! I can't believe I forgot his name. I'll never forget that face though," he says.

"Did you know Jake?"

"Hah! Jake was my neighbor. He'd always harass my mom. One time I told my Dad, and he laid Jake out with one punch! My dad was awesome! That pissed Jake off, and he hated me after that. For months he wouldn't come near our house or even look our way. Then one day he got drunk and kidnapped me as I was walking home from school. He took me out here and drowned me in this swamp."

"You're that missing boy, Daniel?" I ask.

"Yes, that's my name, Daniel! I almost forgot," he answers.

"You've been out here this whole time?" I question.

"Yes. My body was never given a proper burial, so my soul is stuck here until they find me."

Walking over to the area where our bodies were buried, I try to move the leaves but am unable to. Daniel walks over and puts his arm around me, but it falls through not making contact.

"That's impossible!" he says.

"What?"

"I can't touch you. If something's dead I can usually touch it, but you...are...fading!"

"What does that mean?"

"It means you're still alive!"

"We need to wake me up! I have a cell phone in my pocket. I can call for help! Help me wake up, Daniel!" I beg.

He starts walking in circles scratching his head.

"The animals! They can hear us. They can help!"

Running towards my body, Daniel sounds a loud battle cry. Creatures emerge from the swamp and surround my body making loud animal noises. The sound eventually stirs me. My hand begins to move. My body lifts from the ground. Fading fast I find myself back in my body, but I can no longer see Daniel. Pulling my cell phone out of my pocket, I dial and patiently wait as the phone rings. The pain is setting in fast. I don't have much longer. Dizziness sets in, and I fall back. What if I can't get through? Blood pools around me. I might not survive this. But I have to hang on, for Daniel.

"Sherman County Police, what's your emergency?"

"Daniel's body...by the swamp..." I can barely speak. "Route 23...Jake Samson...mur-der-er..."

My hand releases the phone and I can hear talking on the other end as I fade away.

"They'll find us now," said Daniel, holding my hand.

Moments later the sound of an ambulance siren blares in the distance, and the animals sound their sound right back, calling out in our direction.

2

WATER

by
Douglas G. Clarke

The water lapped happily against the roots of a red maple, thankful for the assistance of the passing alligator whose tail brought movement to its stagnant existence. Life had been so exciting in the beginning. Born as ten thousand droplets falling from the sky, dancing down the steep mountainside, it gathered and formed in a clear mountain lake.

Yes, life had been so much more exciting. Since reaching the swamp, everything was slow like the sap crawling down the maple tree's bark. There had been so much hope and anticipation. The salt of the ocean had been in the air and even at times in the water around it. Instead of racing down a turbulent river trying to out pace its siblings, here the others were listless. There was no competition.

More than the slowness, for the water had been ready to spend a season frozen as snow or even longer as a glacier, it was the cloudiness of its mind that disturbed it the most. It had once seen every pebble, every fish, and every bird. Now it couldn't even make out the ground, and only knew that there were frogs around because they swam through it.

It had not been overcome with despair like some of its siblings had. They gave themselves up and dispersed into the remains of those who had given up before. So much of death lay all around it. The maples dropped their dead leaves covering it, the snakes on the shore shed their skins, and the wind added them to the leaves. The alligators killed fish and anything that was unaware enough to enter the stagnate pools.

But the water clung to the hope of the sea—a place of renewal and fellowship, an endless playground of tides and waves and currents. If the sea could be smelled, it couldn't be that far away. So day and night the water tried to move across the vast and unmapped swamp.

The sea had come in, and so there must be a way out or this would be a truly dead place filled with salt, the only escape would be evaporation. No, this was not hell. This was purgatory, a place to get through, a place that the strong and righteous could get through.

But was the water strong or righteous? Its body weakened everyday as it filled with bacteria, silt, algae, and death. And how could it judge whether it was righteous or not? The alternative was death, so the water believed.

Vibration. A growing roar. The screams of death as something split the water and churned it up. Then there was pain as a boat cut across the water's back. The propeller ripped it apart. It was almost more than the water could bear. But as the boat passed and the pain lessened, the water saw an opportunity.

The stagnant swamp was suddenly alive. A path had cut across and water was flowing in to fill the gouge. The water leapt at the chance and flowed in behind the boat, letting its draft pull it along.

The ride did not last long, and the swamp was still vast around it. But it moved. It had hope. It felt its wounds start to heal, and in fact it began to feel better than it had before. The boat had pulled air down into the water and restored some of its youth.

The water felt strange, waiting there and hoping another boat would pass. Waiting for the searing pain again, but knowing that with the pain came health and movement. The wait was long, many days and nights, but the wait was not in vain.

This time when the boat passed the water was ready. It didn't just wait for the boat. It struggled to reach it. This time the pain was even greater, but its planning had allowed it to jump in behind the boat. Swirling and spinning at the stern of the boat, the propeller continually chopped it. The water lost consciousness.

When it woke it found that it was still alive, and more, it was still moving. A gentle current pulled it along. The taste of salt was in its mouth. The water wondered if it was dreaming when it heard the voices of others. But soon, as the others embraced it, it knew that it was home.

3

MAPLE LEAF RAG

by
Laura Stafford

Steve Coxwell leveraged his paddle against the ancient stump to push the little boat out into the murky swamp. He hadn't considered how difficult it would be to navigate the fallen trees and stumps in the dark, but it was too late to turn back now.

He wiped sweat from his brow and looked at the body lying in the front of the boat. It had been over ten years since Steve had seen Dan Harshorne. Today his old football buddy had shown up at the Maple Leaf Rag, Steve Coxwell's bar and grill that had a down-home-on-the-bayou atmosphere with Mardi Gras food.

Thinking back now, what else could he have done? Tackle his old football buddy and stop him from inspecting the kitchen?

* * *

Steve heard the ring of the door from the kitchen. He would have recognized Dan anywhere despite the years. The scar on his chin and his trademark blue eyes made him unmistakable.

"Dan Harshorne? That you? Holy crapola!" Steve wiped his hands on a clean towel and came out of the kitchen.

"Steve! Well, waddayaknow?" They half shook and half hugged the way men do, shoulder-to-shoulder with minimal contact. "This is your place?"

"Ayup. Goin' on ten years now. What you got yerself into? I ain't seen you since prob'ly high school. Let's get you a seat, and I'll fix you up some of my famous frog legs. Specialty of the house!" Steve stood with his large fists on his wide hips surveying Dan. Steve looked smaller and older but still had a quarterback's gleam in his eye. Dan held up his hand.

"I'd love to, but I can't," Dan said, holding out a paper and an I.D. "I'm actually the health inspector now. Just got hired two weeks ago. Unfortunately, I'm here to work."

"Huh. No kidding." Steve rubbed his chin. "Well, have at it then."

After finishing the inspection, Dan shook his head as he approached Steve.

"Chytrid fungus," Dan explained. "Major violation...gotta file a report, probably going to close for quite some time...not sure what will happen...re-inspection. Good thing I didn't let you make me any of those famous frog legs!" Dan laughed jovially.

Steve imploded. He imagined his hands reaching out to strangle Dan, to throttle him till he slumped like a rag doll, to put firecrackers in his mouth that would explode him inside out the way they used to do with the frogs down at the swamp.

Instead Steve smiled. "Not your fault," he told Dan. "Just doin' your job…maybe come by the house for a beer?"

Dan shook his head no, excusing himself to file his report.

Stopping Dan with a heavy hand on his arm, Steve smiled again. "Come on, you can file your report on Monday. It's been over ten years! Just one beer? Maybe toss the ball a little?"

"All right, twist my arm," Dan laughed.

The old cottage down by the swamp was a familiar place where all the guys on the football team had drank hundreds of beers, kissed as many girls as they could, and told stories by the bonfire. They reminisced about old friends, old girlfriends, and unsolved mysteries like *Who stole Marty Fisher's dirt bike? Where did that cheerleader run away to?* and *Are Miss Fitzsimmon's breasts real?*

"I'm sorry about your restaurant," Dan eventually said through a slur of beer breath. "It shouldn't be closed for too long. I hope you have some savings…"

Whatever warmth from memories, Steve felt suddenly dissipated like smoke on the wind. Steve stood and walked behind Dan. "It's okay, Dan. You won't be filing that report." Steve brought a tire iron down into Dan's skull.

* * *

Steve misjudged the middle of the swamp and bumped the boat against a rock, sending something skittering into the water. He rolled Dan's body up and over the side of the boat almost capsizing the whole thing.

Steadying the boat by placing his hands and feet, Steve watched the ripples and rings wave away in the moonlight. Already Dan's body had disappeared into the murk and muck. He tossed the tire iron over the side and sat to calm his thrumming heart.

The swamp would keep his secret.

After all, that cheerleader had never surfaced, and it had been over ten years.

4

THE REUNION

by
Kristen Strassel

"What's the matter? You're too good to come to the reunion?" I didn't even have to swing my barstool around. Even after seven years, that voice hadn't changed. No one else would bother to approach me. It was much more fun for them to whisper to themselves and make up their own stories about me.

"Pretty much."

I turned around anyway and smiled at Jordan Monroe, my high school sweetheart, who stood in almost the exact spot I last left him in when I told him I was moving to New York. I melted a little inside when my eyes met his. I thought I had severed all ties to this place, and I intended to keep it that way.

Jordan slid into the bar seat next to mine and raised his chin to Jackie, the bartender, who just like that knew what to bring over for him. I moved my purse to make room, being careful to miss the sticky drink residue on the wood. This purse hadn't come from the local Wal-Mart.

"Ha, swamp juice!" Jordan called me out before taking a sip of his beer. "Didn't know famous New York actresses drank such things. I figured you'd have a merlot or something."

"I've drank plenty of merlot, but when I'm in Bright Star, I do as the Bright Starians do."

We clinked mason jars and caught up. Maybe it was the juice or the company, but that warm fuzzy feeling of familiarity crept over me, even though I'd promised myself I'd keep my guard up. I was only in town to clean out my aunt's house.

"Let's get out of here," Jordan whispered in my ear two drinks later. I nodded, grabbing my purse and his arm to steady myself on my stilettos after way too much moonshine.

"Those are some fancy shoes," he smiled suggestively. "They don't look like they were made for walking."

"In New York these are practically sneakers." The humid night air covered me like a blanket as we left the tavern. "Plus, when you come to the swamp, you bring your alligators."

"Alligator shoes? Those must have cost a fortune."

"I bought myself a present when I got nominated for an Emmy."

"Yeah, I heard about that. So you can walk in those things?"

"Of course."

Jordan looped out his arm for me just in case, as he led me past the rocky parking lot into the woods. The tavern wasn't far from the old dock we used to party at in high school. Even after years, I knew these woods and paths like I had walked them yesterday. The moon reflected off the swamp lighting our way.

Jordan stopped me in front of an ancient maple tree still debased:

JENNA N JORDAN 4EVA

Even with all this familiarity, it looked like a message in a time capsule. No one had called me Jenna since I left Bright Star. I'd had a hard time answering to it since I'd been back. Maybe that girl was still here with Jordan forever. Still I smiled at Jordan in the moonlight, cherishing the memory when he was enough for me.

"Remember this?" He asked as he leaned me against the tree, his face close to mine.

"I never would forget."

"Listen, there is something I didn't tell you about me back in the tavern."

"What?" I rolled my eyes preparing myself for a declaration of undying love.

"I've changed."

"We all have, Jordan." I couldn't hide my annoyance. "What? Are you gay or something?"

He laughed too loudly, his eyes changing. "Hardly. I may have let you walk away from me once, but I'm not going to do it again. You owe me."

My heart pounded. I was out in the woods alone with a lunatic. "What are you talking about?"

"I threw away my football scholarship for you, and you ran off to New York without me. You ruined my life. You're family didn't die. I killed them, one by one, trying to get your attention. But you were too good for all of them. You only came back here so you could sell your aunt's house. All you care about is money."

"Jordan, that's not true. I couldn't get away." I pleaded between gasps for air.

"You didn't want to." He brushed his rough hand against my face making me shiver.

"That's OK. You'll have plenty of time to catch up with them when you join them in the swamp."

5

BAITING HOLLOW

by
Jot Russell

Within the middle of a brackish swamp at Baiting Hollow Scout Camp was a small wooden house. The abandoned shack was held up from slimy depths, by pilings that were eaten away from years of decay. Remaining deck planks that surrounded the structure were twisted and warped with nail heads extending out. The swamp had swallowed the boardwalk. It had once connected the dirt road to the house.

One day during a walk to the beach, I thought I saw something within one of its broken windows.

"Hey, guys, stop! I think I saw something move in there." I pointed.

Phil, the largest one, said, "Yeah, it's probably the fishman!"

I shook off his tease. "That's just a campfire story that someone made up."

Jim, the eldest one, said, "No, Phil's right. There really was a fisherman who lived in there. They say he had badly scarred hands from cuts he never cleaned.

The infection spread to his body causing his skin to develop scales. Eventually it extended into his mouth and lungs. One day gasping for air, he collapsed into the water and was never seen again. They say he stays down there to breathe but still comes out at night to watch his house.

Phil grabbed me. "Let's send Steve over to take a look."

"No way, I'm not going in there!"

Phil pushed me closer to the edge of the swamp. I struggled but couldn't push back.

As my foot sank into the water, I screamed. "Stop!"

Jim grabbed Phil and pulled him away. "Why don't you go?"

"I'm not walking through that," Phil said.

"Then use a canoe from the lake," Jim directed.

Phil threw a rock and hit the house. "Screw that. I'm going to the beach."

Everyone else followed but Jim. "You okay?"

"Yeah, I'm fine. You really think he's in there?"

"Who knows? Come on, let's get out of here."

Years later the three of us went kayaking on the Long Island Sound near Baiting Hollow. The high tide slowly streamed into the marshy swamp.

"Hey, you guys think that fisherman house is still there?" Jim asked.

I looked over. "Looks like we can paddle in. Let's take a look."

Phil protested. "I don't want to go in there."

Jim followed. "Come on, Phil. You've been to prison. You've had to deal with far worse than a fictional fishman."

Reluctantly Phil followed us in.

We entered the dark marsh as the sun set behind what we called Suicide Hill. It was still and quiet. The only sound was coming from our paddles moving through the water. Not even a peep from a bird or insect. Ahead lay the remains of the house somehow still sitting above the murky waters. I thought we were going to dock and step out onto the deck, but an eerie feeling led me to circle around first. I tried to look inside the holes in the glass, but the black interior gave no view within. I paused and focused my eyes to let them adjust to the darkness. There within a window, a face appeared that seemed like a ghost. It had green scaly flesh and eyes completely white with death. My soul froze as those eyes stared straight into mine.

In the corner of my gaze, I could see Phil coming around drawing ever closer towards a wall. As I was held powerless to warn him, he extended his paddle and broke part of the glass on a side window. Suddenly the fishman disappeared from the window, releasing me from my spell.

"He's in there!" I screamed.

"Very funny," said Phil, not seeing the fishman rise from the water behind him.

I pointed and screamed again. "Look out!"

Phil looked back just in time to see the fishman grab his arm and sink his black teeth into the flesh. Phil screamed and struggled to break free, but the fishman held him still and continued to chew.

Jim paddled up from behind and rammed into the back of the creature. The fishman let go of Phil and turned around to flip over Jim's kayak. Jim went under, but he came back up and stood in the shallow water. The fishman was gone.

I saw Jim pulling something out of his pocket as the scaled hairless head appeared once more.

"Behind you!" I pointed.

Jim swung around and planted his knife into the head of the monster. Jim let go as bloody water gurgled from the creature's lipless mouth slowly submerging lifeless into the water.

6

RIBBIT-RIBBIT
HELP RUN *FROG-FROGS*

by
Richard Bunning

Amongst what Bigfeet call *Red Maple Swamp* is the froggish land of Rana. International peace reigns in this prosperous union of fiefdoms. In recent centuries there has been very little fighting with any territory beyond Rana, or between the races living within its borders. Though, nothing stays the same forever. When serious conflict has occurred, the Ranaians' Supreme Council has usually employ mercenary Cane Toad soldiers to restore order. Relationships between the races, or families, are usually very good, however, relations within families are a different matter. We will come back to this in a moment, but let me first draw the big picture.

Within the boundaries of Rana, there is an abundance of space and food, even at the height of the Summer Metamorphoses, when the schools of young tadpoles graduate. They close their gills, push out their legs, and hop out of the waterways. At these times danger threatens from flying dragons, though luckily few of these can manoeuvre well in the thick stands of Maple. Usually frogs have time to reach safety as their allies, the squirrels, launch anti-bird nut-missiles. In addition land rights have long been given to the lizards in return for keeping Rana free from snakes. All the distant land is regularly attacked by the Plough of the Bigfeet, the very creatures that chopped and burnt most of the frogs ancient forests, and now annually fold over all the land with huge steel blades, burying alive any plant or beast that gets in the way. It seems that beautiful Rana is surrounded by deserts worked by the engines of Hell.

The government, the Council of Rana, is made up of royals of all the families, and is presided over by the Great Salamander, head of the Caudata family. The Cadatas' physically smaller distant cousins, known collectively as the Newts, run the administration, collect insect tax, and own most commercial businesses. So why isn't well ordered Rana always peaceful?

The problem amongst all frog societies is that neither sex is in the least bit monogamous. Indeed constant sexual activity with any Jack or Jill that passes is totally the central ambition of any frog's life. From every fit adult in every corner of Rana there are constant cries of courtship. Just stop and listen to the excited chatter in any frog community; *rabbit-rabbit, ribbit-ribbit, grabit-grabit, quaak-quaak, cooa-cooa, hump-hump, Berp, rabbit*. What a din. The Great Salamander, demands quiet when the sun is high so that everyone can get at least a little sleep. Of course sex is discouraged underwater, so as to protect the innocence of the children in their kindergartens.

As promiscuous sex is the main activity the male frogs are constantly fighting for ladies. A lot of the quarrels are literally fratricidal, brother against brother for the favours of the next available elegant female leg. There is usually official peace between the families, the Sylvaticas, Catesbeianas, Palustris and Heckscheri; but between close neighbours, that's a different matter. Even the strange Crucifers, nomadic travellers on the dryer margins of the Swamp, get along well enough with the other families. Yet they fight like cats amongst themselves.

Things are changing in the New Enlightenment. The Salamanders and the powerful Catesbeianas family have united to force stability and monogamous relations. Society has run by negotiation for hundreds of years, but now military government is slowly imposing its weight on the previously independent. Temporarily there is internecine warfare, as the families are subdued one by one. Lacking the organization of the New Model Army, the rebellious groups inevitably fall like dominoes.

Of course, there will never be complete peace for long unless frog nature can be changed. But society is now increasingly controlled. A new enforced social morality is being established. Soon the frogs will be focusing on expansion beyond Rana's borders, on subduing the Bigfeet. Legions of disciplined frogs sent out, conquistadors, to challenge the course of evolution. For now the anticipation of sweet revenge on the leg-eating Bigfeet is enough to cement the unity of Ranaians. The borrowed battle cry of tropical tree frogs, *Coqui, Coqui,* echoes forth along the borders, as the legions prepare to march. As the frogs learn to funnel the energy of courtship into conquest, all the creatures of Earth will shudder with fear. The cry of alarm, *Frogs, Frogs,* will soon be echoing across the Earth. Ploughshares will be turned into guns, but will that be enough to save the demonic Bigfeet? History will tell.

7

AIZAWA TAVERN

by
Alli Vaughan

Though sections of land rose out of the water, they mostly plodded through festering mud and climbed over roots upturned in long tapered rows.

"Hakle owns Aizawa Tavern," Ryn said, lifting his slime-coated boot. "It's him we have to convince."

"Does he speak Japanese?" Hugo asked with a sigh, as he shooed a blanket of swamp flies bombing his head with his thick hand.

"No," Ryn replied. "He speaks English, so you can just enjoy the sake."

Hugo grunted in reply. Ryn smiled. His old friend had held up pretty well these last few days, trudging through the tar like swamps of Tasek Bera, Japan's black water swamp lake located in the southern part of Malay Peninsula. Hugo had only come along as an interpreter for Ryn, but after everything they had been through, the man needed a night off. And a night to appreciate the tavern's unique servers, Hakle's geishas.

"All this to save a blasted tree," he heard Hugo grumble under his thick beard after several minutes.

"Not just any tree, Hugo. The Scarlet Spider Maple species has almost died out. This swamp holds the last trees of its kind, and they are all infected. If we can't get Hakle to help us, they are done for."

"You're sounding like a tree hippy anymore, Ryn," Hugo said.

"Dendrologist," Ryn corrected. "I've told you hundreds of times, I'm a tree scientist."

"Same thing," Hugo replied.

"The road is just up ahead, it's a chance to get out of this mire."

The road cleaned the muck of their steps as they proceeded. A lanky bridge escorted them through the tree line to the tavern. Aizawa Tavern wore cheap decorations slapped onto the exterior, decaying against the backdrop of the swamp. A gold and red paper dragon rotted in the humidity near the entrance. Ryn swung the thin door open, greeting them to the smell of curry and sweat.

"Ryn Elbrer!" a thin man with beady eyes shouted from across the room.

"Hakle!"

"And this is?" Hakle asked, sizing up the large man at Ryn's side.

"My speech specialist," Ryn said, knowing the title would irk Hugo. "His throat is dry, can you parch it?"

"Of course! Ming, sake for my friends!"

A geisha bowed and fetched drinks.

"So why are you here? Not that I'm complaining." Hakle stared unblinking.

"We're here about the Spider Maples," Ryn said.

"Oh?" His body seemed to stiffen.

"Yes, the species is dying out. We actually came here to see if we could stay here a month and study the trees on your property. You own hundreds of acres, and most of the species are on your land. With a little time, we can figure out how to reseed the population and see them flourish again."

"That's an interesting proposal, Ryn. Give me a moment to fetch something that'll help me decide."

"Fetch something?" Ryn asked suspiciously.

"Yes, it'll only be a moment," the thin man said, disappearing into the back.

"His eyes," Hugo whispered.

"I noticed," Ryn replied. Hakle's pupils split vertically down the center instead of curving into a circular human eye. His old friend had changed.

"Well, I just can't help you, Ryn," Hakle said, walking back. His demeanor had changed.

"I just can't help you at all." The glint of his sword caught in the low light of the room.

"Why not?" Ryn asked, a chill gripping his spine. The words had scarcely left his mouth when four geishas emerged from the back of the tavern carrying bright daggers. They glided across the floor, bolting the door and blocking their exit.

Hugo struggled against a geisha who tried to bind his arms. The raven-haired woman slammed the hilt of her dagger to the back of the big man's head, knocking him unconscious.

"What's the meaning of this?" Ryn asked angrily.

"You see, the trees you want to save are kept alive by a secret. The Kayrug frog lives in the trunk and secretes a special substance from its skin. Without those frogs, the trees die."

"What does that have to do with you, Hakle? Why are you doing this?"

"I have a very special diet now that I've sold my spirit living these years in the swamp," Hakle said. A thin tongue darted out of his mouth.

"The frogs!" Ryn realized.

"Yes!" Hakle cackled. "And the occasional human, when he stumbles into my den. And don't worry, we can keep the trees alive without a scientist poking around our swamp."

8

ENSLAVED: 1831

by
Harry Alexiou

Amos Hardy was tied to a Red Maple. He screamed out again as his master, Mr. Wiles, let loose with the merciless whip of a strong sapling. It was Wiles' favourite method for *correctional teaching* as he put it. Amos' only crime was speaking out against the lack of food after his master had berated him and the others for not working hard enough, for slacking off. His comment at the time seemed brave, as the others had gasped at his outburst. Now it just seemed foolish. He looked up at the supervisor's shack with its smoking chimney high on the mound and longed to be warming himself by the log fire that burned inside. Another lash hit home. He re-shifted his focus to the grim reality of his pitiful existence and of his endless suffering. He was sure he would die right there in the Great Dismal Swamp.

The pain seemed to be more bearable now. The *teaching* was almost over. He counted the last of the lashes. The bindings were all that prevented him from collapsing to the ground. Then the axe swung menacingly cutting him loose. Amos Hardy dropped heavily to the damp woodland floor. He shivered and felt cold.

"Think long and hard next time before y'open yer mouth to me, boy!" Wiles yelled out as he made his way back up to the warmth of his shack.

Wiles was in charge of the canal digging project and happy to watch the enslaved workforce making him rich. The lumber produced by the canal dig was a decent earner for Wiles. He was skimming off plenty for himself. Knowing that the company had no idea as to the exact number of trees felled, he only told them what he wanted them to hear. *Give the owner a reasonably high number, and they'll never know.*

The workforce struggled waist deep in water and fought all manner of insects, snakes, and bugs. As long as their heads were above water, then they worked. Any slackers received a correction lesson from an overseer— usually from Wiles. On this day and for some time to come, the screams from Amos Hardy would be remembered.

Marta heard the pained cries of Amos, her eldest. As she worked with the others, her sad despairing eyes released the tears she tried to hold back. It did no good to cry but when she did it made her feel human in this inhumane existence. She pictured the innocent face of Ben, her youngest, who was sold to the Wilmot family for four hundred dollars two weeks ago. Marta's tortured mind recalled the forced sale. *What fate would befall him at the hands of the drunken Master Wilmot?*

Moses, her middle son, had run off in search of berries and whatever food he could glean from the swamp yesterday. His promise of catching a Yellow-Bellied Turtle seemed cruelly insignificant now. They argued before he ran off and she regretted her harsh tone—praying to God that it would not be their final exchange. With a heavy heart she awaited his return, but hope was fading for the young boy's safety. He had most certainly ventured into an area populated by rebels, the worst criminal element of the swamp. The rebels lived in so called *freedom* but were marooned in secretive communities among the dense underbrush.

Amos felt relieved, as he lay motionless on the ground. He flinched as a cold hand touch his shoulder. "Be still, my son." Marta was permitted to tend his wounds as best as she could, all the while glancing around the woods for her lost son. Amos interrupted her thoughts.

"Mother," his rasping voice was slow and deliberate. "Fear not...I will continue to chop wood at night...to sell...I will make enough to buy our freedom...you'll see." He winced as she continued cleansing his wounds.

"My son, you are in no state to chop anything... let us pray again tonight for the safe return of your brother." She currently cared not for freedom but for the lives of loved ones, be it free or enslaved. As the tears rolled unabated down her soft dark skin, she was glad that Amos faced away from her. His pain had been enough for one day.

That evening as Marta recited her prayers and settled down for five hours of sleep before sunrise and the next shift, she heard a rustling outside the shelter. Her heart skipped a beat, but she knew it was Moses before she even set eyes on the bedraggled figure.

"Mother, didn't I say I would get you a Yellow-Bellied Turtle?"

"Oh, my Lord!" She cried with arms wide and her head raised to the heavens.

OLD ELLERBE

by
Oliver Dolan

When Great Grandfather Indigo moved to the states just after the turn of the century, he purchased some property in the Florida swampland not too far from the gulf. He built a humble cottage, acquired a fishing boat, and began hunting and selling alligators to local restaurants.

He took a liking to the intimidating creatures and fed them small mammals when they crawled out of the swampy water. He eventually planted maple trees all around the cottage and down by the water to beautify his estate. He used a combination of vitamins to make sure they grew fast, and concocted a special formula using herbs, swamp water, and gator feces for one special tree that he planted at the edge of the swamp.

The cottage had been mostly vacant since his death. My parents renovated it in the early eighties, and they used it to get away from the tourist trap of a city in central Florida. Later on I took trips to the cottage with my wife at the time and our son, Ignacious.

Alexis left me a few years back for my old college roommate, Ronnie. They worked together at the local university and had a close hold on Ignacious ever since. Feeling broken and ashamed after our divorce was official, I quit my job and moved into the cottage.

The gators came by to say hello like they had been for a hundred years. Occasionally my neighbor, Lenny, would join me for breakfast.

"Hey, Italo," Lenny said as we enjoyed our bacon and eggs on the front porch one morning. "Your dad ever tell ya about Old Ellerbe?"

"Uh... no. Who's that?" I asked.

"Well, see that big old maple tree down there? Right by the water?"

"Yeah, what about it?"

"I'm sure ya know that Great Granddaddy Indigo planted that there tree. Maybe ya even know how he got it to be so darn big. A few of the locals say that it's the biggest gator they've ever laid their eyes on. It lives in there. They say she's been around for years now, weighs a couple thousand pounds, and she don't take kindly to strangers."

"Oh, yeah? How's she get in there? It doesn't look like there's a hole big enough to fit a thousand pound gator."

"They tell me it's some type of force field or somethin'. It's kinda like the tree and Ellerbe are pals."

We finished our breakfast in silence, and I didn't spend another minute thinking about a fictitious gator that *lives* inside the giant maple tree.

Alexis called me one morning and asked if she and Ronnie could drop Ignacious off the week before Christmas while they went to see Ronnie's parents. I replied with an emphatic *yes*, and looked forward to seeing my son for the first time in months.

I watched from a distance as they pulled up in one of those luxury SUVs. Ignacious hopped out of the back seat and came running up to me. He thrust himself into my arms.

"Daddy! Daddy! So good to see you! I wish I could come all the time and watch the gators and just relax."

"I know. Same here. I love you. It's great to see you."

"Plus, I hate Ronnie. He's always really mean to me and mommy." He whispered as they approached.

I traded artificial pleasantries with Alexis while Ronnie put Ignacious's bags inside. Ronnie walked right past me like I didn't even exist. Alexis, Ignacious, and I walked inside and watched through the back window as Ronnie headed down to the dock to get a view of the swamp. I felt my blood boiling with anger at the thought of how everything went down, but somehow I was still able to have a casual conversation with my ex.

As I looked at Alexis, I saw something moving rapidly out of the corner of my eye. I turned. The three of us watched as an incredibly large alligator severed

Ronnie's legs and dragged his body into the water. Old Ellerbe, I think, it must have been!

I ran outside while the two of them screamed. Alexis reached for her phone to call 911. Blood splattered across the dock and on top the water. Quickly emerging from the mess, Ellerbe scared me stiff. The gator paused, spit out a finger with what looked like a wedding band, and ran directly into the maple tree. It seemed to swallow Ellerbe whole.

I heard sirens in the distance as Ignacious came to my side.

"Well, son…I guess I'll be seeing a lot more of you now."

10

TESSA ROSEWOOD
& THE
GREEN RIVER
by
H. M. Schuldt

Tessa Rosewood couldn't stand it anymore. Several small town folks in Green River, Louisiana, were saying terrible things about her best friend, Valerie. There must be some other explanation for Valerie's disappearance other than running away.

Valerie did not run away! Tessa slammed the front door and went out for an afternoon jog.

Two peas in a pod, Tessa and Valerie were best friends. They had recently finished their sophomore year with plans to travel to Europe as part of a special program for honor students.

Tessa jogged nine blocks to get out of the small town and passed by Green River High School. She slowed down in the park and took a walk near Moss Bridge, noticing a Great Blue Heron standing on the other side of the bayou.

"Tessa!" Troy La Salle caught up with his girlfriend. "Have you heard from Valerie?"

"No. It's not like her to disappear," Tessa said. She noticed that he was carrying rope again. "I just saw her yesterday."

"Do you think she ran away with Victor?" Troy asked.

"Don't say that," Tessa replied.

Tessa and Troy walked the entire disc golf course in a hurry.

Making a return back to the bridge, Tessa noticed her cell phone was missing. They walked the course a second time. Troy called her number, and they listened for a ring.

Nothing.

At the ninth hole they finally heard a ring from far away. Some creature must have carried it off the course deep into the swamp. They followed the ring that led them to an oak tree near the bay. Standing at the foot of the tall tree, they heard a ring come from way up high.

"I'll get it," Troy said, beginning to tie a few knots. He made a harness, put on a pair of gloves, and climbed up the oak tree. Reaching out on a high branch, he came eye to eye with a lizard as he retrieved the phone from its mouth. Off in the distance, he thought he saw a figure on the other side of the bay. *You've got to be kidding! Is that Valerie?* Climbing down with Tessa's phone, he told her about what he saw.

"A person?" she asked.

"I don't know," Troy answered. "Let's go check."

They climbed into the groundkeeper's boat and sailed across Black Bay until they arrived at the location where he had seen the figure.

Tessa saw exactly what she didn't want to see. There sitting down leaning against a maple tree was Valerie tied to a trunk. Tessa gasped and felt shivers down her spine.

"Valerie!" Tessa yelled.

Together Troy and Tessa untied Valerie.

"Who did this to you?" Troy asked, helping her up.

"Victor," she whispered.

"That scum!" Tessa scolded.

"No. It was only supposed to be a game. It's Milton's fault. Milton found us having a good time. Milton must have been jealous. He went crazy. Victor punched him. They fought. Victor passed out. Milton took him away in his jeep. You have to find Victor," Valerie pleaded.

"Okay," Troy agreed. "Let's go."

Valerie was dehydrated and feeling weak in the car. Troy drove the two girls to a corner shop—the only one in town—so they could get a drink of water.

"You happen to see a jeep pass by?" Troy asked Dan, the cashier who regularly had grubby fingernails.

Dan happened to be the small town mechanic who also happened to be the cashier as well as the corner shop owner.

Handing Dan a five-dollar bill, Troy bought two waters and a coke.

"Yep. It was crazy Milton. He's trouble," Dan said. "They locked up his daddy for trying to rob a bank. His mom ran off, and now he lives with his dad's weirdo brother. You stay away from that boy. He's nothing but trouble."

"Have a good one," Troy left the corner shop and drove straight out to Milton's house.

Troy pulled down Milton's long driveway. It had been covered up with overgrown bushes for years. There near the old two-story house was Milton's jeep. Troy sprang out of his car, landing on the dirt.

"Milton!" Troy yelled up the porch steps. "You get out here right now!"

It was silent.

Then Milton opened the front door and stepped out on to the porch next to a broken rocking chair.

"You got a problem, ya couyon? Get out of my yard!" Milton snarled.

"Get down here! What'd ya do with Victor?" asked Troy.

"Don matta." Milton scoffed wiping boudin from his mouth.

Troy stormed over to Milton's jeep.

"You get away from my jeep!" Milton yelled. He flew down the wood steps and jumped on Troy's back.

Troy threw him onto the ground. Milton rose and lunged at him. Troy landed him a strong punch. Milton fell to the ground again and passed out. That's when Victor broke free from a shed.

"Let's put him in your car!" Victor fled forward with vengeance.

They placed Milton in Troy's car and drove back to the same maple tree where Valerie had been found. Zydeco music filled Troy's car, *Hello Rosa Lee* by Clifton Chenier.

"I'll get the rope." Victor seemed out of control.

Sometime after Milton was tied to the maple tree, he woke up.

"Hey!" Milton growled. He struggled to get loose but couldn't.

Victor grinned. Four high school kids returned to Troy's car and drove away.

"How long are we going to leave him out there?" Tessa asked.

"At least one night." Valerie wanted justice.

"Let him rot out there forever." Victor had no mercy.

"We'll send the police to get him ... tomorrow."

At sunrise Troy called the police.

11

THE SWAMP TRADER

by
Randy Dutton

"Hallo!" The hunched man called out to anyone beyond the south gate swamp picket. He glanced left and right to the entangled vine maple barricade mostly encircling the sodden refuge. The maples were planted generations ago. Thin strong branches were woven together like prison bars to make an impenetrable barrier.

"State your business, mutant!" the teenage guard challenged. His steel-tipped arrow was aimed at the grizzled man's chest.

"Name's Girth. Just doin' a bit of tradin' with me pal, Munk, at the Swamp Violet Inn. Got some jerked wild beef in me pack. Thought I swap fer some metal work and a tad of sanity."

"Put down the crossbow, lad. He's a regular," the older guard said.

The leather-clad visitor in his early forties shuffled through the gateway, the demarcation between opposing worlds.

"You know the drill, trader. Hang your pack. Then shower and step forward."

The man slung his canvas bag onto a hook hanging from a rope looped between trees. As the pack was winched to the guard post, the trader walked under the deerskin bladder, pulled the cord, and was rewarded with a cascade of cold soapy water. "Brrrrrr. Ye washin' the mold off me sure dunna make a fella feel welcome!"

"It was your choice to visit, trader." The older guard inspected the contents while the other lowered his bow. "You got any sunflower seeds or plants in your kit?"

"Nope," Girth said, shaking excess water from his long tangled hair. He used an old towel hanging from a tree branch to wipe his bearded face.

"Been awhile since I had me some beef," the seasoned guard said.

"Take a piece fer ye and the young-un." The trader grinned mischievously.

"Thanks. Think I will," the older guard said, then closed the canvas pack. "Looks okay."

"How are the drylands?" the younger guard asked.

"No change. Sunflowers everywhere. Yer lucky sunflowers dunna grow in dark wet swamps. The ergot mold be powerful as ever, blowing off, and gittin' into their food. The druggies always be under its power. They kill and eat anything, so I keeps me distance."

"We've been expecting them to attack. If they're so doped up, how do you trade with them?"

"Ye must be new. I wait until they be so wasted they canna fight. And they no remember much, so I git good trade."

"Looks like the sunflower mold has some impact on you," the guard said, noting his pallor and sunken eyes.

"I be fifth generation, born in a drug prison before the druggies kilt off most people. The plague don't affect me mind none." Girth hoisted his heavy pack onto his shoulders. "Be fer, I always enter from the north gate. How fer be the Inn?"

"Two miles along the main cypress swamp road. Move along then."

Arriving at the cypress log-hewn inn, the trader glanced at the carved signboard hanging above the door. Its five-petaled violet blossom symbolized the dark dank world where sunflowers wouldn't grow, and the hallucinogenic mold spores hadn't infiltrated. Inside the inn the militia was having dinner. Girth entered and dropped his pack onto the bar. "Munk, I gots some tradin' to do with ye."

A tall slim man looked into the bag. "Long time, ol' friend. May I?"

Girth nodded approval. "Ye all kin have a taste," he announced loudly and revealed a sly grin as he handed samples to the refuge's militia.

The armed men eagerly chewed the flavorful meat.

Munk handed Girth a mug of moonshine and started chewing a piece. They chatted for half an hour about how the druggies coveted the swamp's metalworking resources, particularly the weapons.

The innkeeper spoke softly. "Some swampers say traders aren't to be trusted."

"I be of both worlds." Girth glanced at the tavern patrons and his grin grew. Some were becoming dizzy gesturing wildly.

Just then the young guard staggered in. His head was bleeding. "They're attacking!" He fell onto the floor as crazed-eyed men with knives and clubs swarmed past him into the tavern, attacking the drug-stupefied militia.

Some militiamen stumbled for weapons. Their uncoordinated movements doomed them. Others hid under tables crying out in despair, "We're gonna die!"

Munk was dizzy. He spit out the remains of the jerky. "Girth, what have you done?"

"I soaked me jerky in ergot tainted broth. The druggies want yer metal weapons, but yer militia be in the way. I want the swamp. As I said, I make good trade."

12

EVANGELINE

by
Gail Harkins

The article was buried on page twenty-four of the newspaper, *Glowing Frogs Infest Bayou,* but to Dr. Jamie Chartier, it leapt out. "Dr. Furneaux, perhaps?"

Her colleague shrugged across a bank of computers. "He inserted the gene encoding for luciferase into zebrafish before he was dismissed, so why not?"

"Luciferase is the enzyme that makes fireflies glow." Jamie smiled. "I asked him to do that to a bonsai maple once. He called it a waste of resources."

Dr. Marcus Hertog gave a huff. "Looks like he has time now."

"That or he's continuing his work. I guess some of his subjects escaped."

"So call the Center for Disease Control," Marcus said as a computer beeped. It registered a hit in the database of a single nucleotide polymorphism.

Jamie nodded. She dialed the airlines instead.

The waning moon cast pale shadows through the moss-shrouded trees. Marcus crouched at the edge of the dirt road. A meter from the swamp, he fixated upon sounds he couldn't identify, sounds that made him shiver despite the heat. When Jamie touched his shoulder, he jumped.

"Shush." She pointed to a distant stand of cypress. "Over there."

Marcus's eyes struggled in the darkness. Finally the light flickered again. "Got it. Let's go."

They stepped into the johnboat, and Marcus pushed off.

"More to the left," Jamie directed. Her skin crawled as if a hundred sets of eyes were upon her waiting. When the small boat rocked, she screamed.

"What?"

"Something's in the water. There! Alligators?"

Marcus's shoulders bunched. "Probably just a log." His voice was clipped. When the oars dipped into the water again, they splashed.

Rounding a bend in the swamp, they saw a small cabin set on stilts and a dock that extended six meters into the water. A kerosene lantern hung from a piling.

"Bonjour, mes amis!" A figure stood to one side. A broad-brimmed hat shadowed his face. "The bayou's dangerous especially at night. Y'all know your way around?"

Jamie turned to Marcus, whispering.

"We're looking for someone, a friend."

"A friend, you say?"

Marcus cleared his throat. "A colleague actually. Dr. Andres Furneaux. Do you know of him?"

The man turned to walk away but stopped when Jamie spoke.

"Andres? It's you, isn't it? It's me, Jamie. Let us dock. As you said, the bayou's dangerous. I don't want to become gator bait."

"Should've thought of that before you got in the boat!" he replied, but he caught the line Marcus tossed and cleated it off.

They walked to the dark cabin in silence. Inside, the only light was a four-meter long plank that glowed along the far wall. As Jamie watched, it moved.

"Stand still, you two," Dr. Furneaux cautioned. He took a chicken carcass from the refrigerator and tossed it through the door into a pen behind the cabin. The alligator sauntered after it.

"Andreas, what have you done?"

"Evangeline is a big one. A gator that size, I want to keep an eye on."

Marcus eyed the glowing mass consuming the chicken. "So you expanded your research to alligators? And frogs?"

"They took away my funding," Dr. Furneaux complained. "I was so close to curing cancer. Then my patient died. He knew gene therapy was risky, but everyone blamed me as if I'd done something wrong!"

"You rushed the trials," Jamie murmured.

"Of course I rushed! He had stage four glioblastoma!" Andreas's widened eyes refocused. "Now I have other funding."

"From where?" Jamie asked cautiously.

"Irrelevant." He brushed the question away. "Besides, clinical trials have already begun."

"You have FDA approval?" Marcus asked.

Jamie noticed the flash in Andreas's eyes and cut in. "You're treating yourself, aren't you?"

Marcus scowled disgusted, but Jamie took the scientist's arm and walked him away. "You're so brave continuing your work here in the bayou. Tell me all about it."

Dr. Furneaux preened at Jamie's praise, and began to discuss his experiments. "I couldn't humanize the amphibian antibody successfully, but when I switched to alligators, I found another option. Rather than humanize an antibody, I created a transgenic alligator that expresses a potent anticancer enzyme in her saliva."

"It works?" Jamie asked.

He tapped his head. "Stage three glioblastoma. Cured." He opened a drawer and handed her a PET scan. "Evangeline is my proof of concept."

The enormity of his words stunned them. Then a point of light caught Jamie's eye, and she turned to the window. The glowing form of Evangeline left barely a ripple as she disappeared into the swamp.

13

MYSTICAL SWAMP

by
Sylvia Stein

In the middle of the Bayou deep in the heart of the town of St. Clare, Louisiana, an old swamp was thought to be mystical. This was due to the strange vision of what they said was a mermaid. They called her Arissa, and she only came out at night when she thought she was needed. In the midst of the swamp where sounds of frogs croaked loudly and other amphibians lurked around, there was one doctor, Dr. Levitan, who was only out to do evil.

Dr. Levitan had already been known to hurt a few of his own patients and had at least one malpractice lawsuit under his belt for transforming a Georgian man into a mutant. The doctor clearly denied any wrongdoing, but he had caused the man to grow snake like skin, and the man was gradually growing worse. This is why the doctor had fled to the small town and was hiding in a small cottage under another name. Dr. Levitan called himself by only one name, Steve, and acted as one of the keepers of the swamp. He raked the leaves that had from time to time been gathered all over the outers of the muddy area. The doctor was thought to not be over his evil ways. He was just trying to stop calling attention to himself, so he figured by acting as a hired hand he would most definitely accomplish his goal.

On the other side of the swamp when all was dark and silent, the mystical mermaid came out. She tried not to make a sound. The last thing she wanted was to be caught. Since she had already seen Steve, she stayed a little above the creek on the side of the muddy swamp. Her tail became legs as she gracefully stepped out of the creek and walked into the very dark swamp. The glistening of magical lights surrounded her. Arissa was a shimmer of joy and light anytime she came out. Her spirit was a gentle one. Although she could not speak, she could produce serene sounds that made everything calm.

Inside his cottage, Dr. Levitan awoke in a sudden pile of sweat feeling dehydrated.

Oh my, this feels just so horrible, he thought to himself. *Why am I so thirsty now?* He quickly walked over to the pitcher on the counter in his small kitchen and drank a glass of water.

He could breathe again.

Suddenly, he was overtaken by the sounds coming from outside. *Why, what could that be?* He gasped. As he stepped outside, Steve saw a beaming flash of blue lights all over the creek that extended from the old swamp to his cottage.

All of this is so surreal, he thought to himself. He did not know why he suddenly felt a need to repent for all the evil he had once caused and for all the evil he thought about trying to do again. As tears streamed through his eyes, a vision of Alissa the mermaid began to emerge before him.

"You are real!" exclaimed the doctor. Thankfully this time, he was not filled with his evil thoughts and ways. Instead he watched her return to the creek, and he saw her swim as she spread all her shimmering lights. He smiled and remembered that it was Christmas Eve. *Well, this is better, than any Winter Wonderland.* Not once in the last five years had he been able to feel good about the holidays.

Could this be my chance to maybe put the past behind and try to live a better life?

"Oh goodness, I really need to try and do some good for the people here in St. Clare. After all I did in my life and those I hurt, this is my second chance!" He shrugged.

There in the muddiest area was a message spelled out in bright lights.

Welcome, Dr. Levitan
Hope you will stay!

This really is a mystical swamp! He smiled from ear to ear and listened to the serene sounds of the mermaid.

For the first time in a long time, Dr. Levitan knew that he was finally home.

14

PRODIGAL SON

by
Lynette White

The horse spooked as the creature rushed him, so Father Laitin Pery dug deep in the saddle. He touched the amulet nestled in the hollow of his throat and quickly recited the prayer. Flame shot from his hand, and the creature's hideous scream made him cringe.

Goblins closely resembled walking toads with crude arms and hands. They lived here in the southern swamps, were of limited intelligence, and had an appetite for horses.

Laitin slipped from the saddle and spoke reassuring words to the horse to calm him down. He was certain that they were alone. The senior priest touched the amulet that hung from his neck and turned his palm up to look at it. Suddenly the figure of a goblin moved in the trees near the road. Scavengers would tend to it from there.

One hour later he arrived at the run down tavern on the edge of the swamp. He went to the stable where a man dressed in simple cotton shorts was brushing down a horse. The groomer scanned the priest from head to foot with raised eyebrows. The heat was oppressive and, despite the fact Laitin was dressed in a red tunic and long black pants, he looked comfortable. The groomer's eyes settled on the dove and sword embossed amulet.

"You are a long way from home, Father," he remarked and nodded at the horse. "It's not smart to ride alone in these parts. You're lucky the goblins didn't snatch your mount right out from under you."

"They made three attempts at it." Laitin stated with a sheepish grin and flipped him a coin before going inside.

The tavern consisted of one room with sparsely placed furniture. Two men sat at one table and a third was snoring in the corner on the floor. Laitin shook his head.

"Of course he is the drunk one," muttered Laitin.

He walked to the man in the corner and kicked him in the stomach with just enough force to get a reaction. "Wake up!"

The man snorted awake and looked up through blurry eyes. "Whoever you are leave me alone," he growled.

Laitin squatted down and curled up his nose. The man reeked of liquor. "I have something for you, Asa."

The man started at the sound of his given name and tried to focus on the stranger beside him. "How do you know my name?"

"Maybe if you chose not to desert me twelve years ago, I would not be a complete stranger to you." Laitin stated and stood up. "But I know you."

Asa Pery struggled to sit up. "Laitin?" He whispered. "Is that really you?"

Laitin reached into his pocket, pulled out a necklace, and dangled it in front of Asa. The chain was delicate, and the charm's emblem was similar to the amulet around his neck.

"Of course it is me, and I have wasted three weeks trying to find you so I could keep a promise and give you this."

Asa took it from him. He stared at it as a profound sadness engulfed him. "Then she is…" he started to say and looked at Laitin. "When?"

"Forty-five days ago. I buried her under the maple tree you planted for her just as she wanted. Mother always prayed you would come back home," explained Laitin.

Laitin stopped and helped Asa into a chair. A long silence followed as Asa quietly wept for his lost mother. When the tears slowed Laitin continued.

"In her final hours mother purged her soul. She told me about the deposits you put in her bank account to keep the roof over our heads. And she told me about your late night visits, so I never knew you were there."

He paused to gather his courage.

"She also told me the truth about Father's murder, how you had to choose between killing him or watching him kill her. I know you were acquitted of the crime, but yet you insisted you had to leave."

Asa stared at the table for several moments. "Yes, I saved mother's life that night. He would never hurt us again, but as I stared at that bloody knife I changed." He continued to explain and finally looked up.

"You were still young and had a chance to end up good." Asa stopped and looked away. "She tried to save me, but I am too broken and corrupt to be saved."

Laitin touched him on the arm. "Nothing is beyond faith and love. I see miracles happen every day to people who are broken just like you. It is time to come home, Asa."

15

SWAMP ISLAND

by
Janet Bond

Betty and I ventured out of Florida on a small boat toward Swamp Island. It wasn't really a big island but rather a small island with a swamp on it. We had heard legends about mermaids living there and wanted to see if they were true.

The boat ride was pleasant enough and the captain let us off at a small dock, making sure to remind us to be here at the same time the following Saturday. We walked up the small dock and onto the beach that was surrounded by tall trees—Red Maples, Aspens, and Black Willows.

We followed a trail that led through the trees hiding the sun from view. Along the sides of the path stood muddy water. We heard frogs crocking and saw a few lizards on the upper branches basking in the sun. The path weaved between the trees and turned when it reached the swamp. There it became a wooden walkway built on posts sunk into the mud.

It wasn't long before our destination came into view. There along the edge of the swamp—which was more like a lake—stood five white cottages and one large building. We walked to the larger building and went in. Inside it was warm and pleasant.

After getting our keys, we went to our cottage. It was beautiful with two small beds on either side of a lace-covered window. The room was lit by a pair of oil lamps, and two over stuffed chairs called out for us to rest in them. The pictures on the Internet hadn't done it justice.

After an afternoon of sitting in those wonderful chairs and listening to the birdcalls drifting on the wind, we decided it was time to get something to eat. We went back to the main building. The Bayou Restaurant had five tables in the back corner. The waitress who owned the hotel greeted us.

"I hope you're having a good time so far. Can I recommend the frog legs? They're fresh and local."

We ate our frog legs, which—just as everyone says—tasted like chicken. After dinner we went for a walk around the lake. Half way around we came to a little park. Isn't that always where things happen—half way around? The park was really just some grass under an old maple tree, but someone had mowed the grass and raked up part the leaves.

Betty apparently couldn't stand seeing all the leaves. She grabbed the rake leaning against the tree and raked the new leaves into the old pile. I sat on the bench waiting. Betty joined me when she was done, and we watched the lake as the sun started to go down.

We noticed some waves lapping the small beach and both wondered how there could be waves on such a small lake. That's when we heard the splash. We looked and saw what looked like a giant fish with arms jump out of the water making another loud splash.

We were excited but a little scared at the same time. We decided that since it was dark, we should get back to our cottage. Flashlights in hand we started down the walkway.

We heard another splash closer in front of us. Then we heard a thump like a body hitting the ground. We stopped when we saw a mermaid lying on the walkway holding herself up with two arms.

We ran the other way past the bench, and then we heard another thump in front of us. We ran back to the park and watched in horror as two more mermaids pulled themselves towards us.

We just kept backing up as they came slowly forward. Then my back hit the trunk of a maple tree. "Climb," I yelled. We climbed as fast and as high as we could. The mermaids circled the tree but didn't try to climb it. Near dawn they went back into the lake. When we were sure they were gone, we climbed down and went back to the cottage.

We spent the rest of the week there, but we made sure we were always in our room before dark. We didn't see the mermaids again, but late at night we knew that they were the ones making the splashes outside our windows.

16

BUBBA

by
Colleen Sayre

Bubba sat on the edge of the old dock, his head in his hands. He'd tried everything he could think of to smuggle Luther safely out of the swamp, everything but emptying his store of fifty-five gallon barrels of gas into the sludgy water and setting it on fire. That wouldn't work either, he knew. When the fire went out, the gators would still be lurking just under the water. The pythons would ease right back in through the smoke and take up residence in their den under the maple tree.

Bubba hated that evil tree! He even tried to cut it down once upon a time, but the county stopped him. They declared it was the oldest living tree in Mohawk County.

"It's not old! That thing's evil!" Bubba yelled when the sheriff showed up. A chainsaw was pried from Bubba's hands. Bubba had stayed away from the tree ever since, but he could hear its whisper from across the swamp. The leaves rustled late at night. It mocked him, and called to him. Tonight he had more important things on his mind. He had to find a way to save Luther!

Luther wasn't speaking to Bubba because Luther had enough of Bubba's games. Luther had been pushed and pulled and forced to do things he didn't want to do. Bubba had asked Luther to ferry a disgusting vial of green liquid out to the center of the swamp and drop it in the water. Bubba wanted to poison the whole swamp to kill the tree. Luther hesitated. He didn't want to be a part of something nefarious. Luther didn't want anyone to know he and Bubba were still friends. But they were friends. *And when my friend needs a favor, I just gotta do it— whatever it is*, thought Luther. Besides Bubba had saved his butt more than once.

So Luther hauled his own skinny butt out through the reeds and the muck and the mud and dropped the little glass container smack in the middle of the swamp.

Deed done! Now, we're even, he thought as he skedaddled home. *Now, we're quits! No more doin' whatever Bubba needs doin'. I'm done! Yeah, right!*

* * *

Lottie was a busybody. She always seemed to know what was going on around the swamp, and she'd seen Luther head out that night with a nervous twitch. She flitted from tree to tree following at a safe distance. She'd seen Luther drop the vial into the water. She saw him take off in a hurry and knew that something wicked was afoot. Lottie passed word to her friends who lived along the edges of the swamp, and they passed the news on to their friends. Her friends found the vial before it spread, and they buried it deep. They had saved the swamp.

Bubba was a skinner and a poacher, and Lottie couldn't abide a man who used his friends for his evil deeds. Poor Luther was a loner—always had been—but for some reason he looked up to Bubba. "Just a poor judge of character," Lottie tried to explain to the croc enforcers when they showed up at her house the next day. "Try to give him a break if you can."

"Oh, we'll give him a break all right!" The enforcers reasoned. Then they lit out for the swamps to look for Luther.

"We'll catch them two together," Big Croc said. "Just you wait and see."

"What are we gonna do about Bubba?" Little Croc asked.

"Oh, he'll get his," Big Croc answered. "It's Luther that we're after. He knows better than to turn on his own. He's a swamp critter like us."

Little Croc hurried to catch up, stretching his short legs as far as they would go. "Why'd ya think he try to poison that old tree, Big Croc? What's it ever done to him?"

"I heard tell years and years ago that they hanged his daddy from that tree."

"Oh, but why does he want to poison the whole swamp?"

* * *

"They're coming for us, Luther. I can feel it." Bubba panicked as water swirled at the end of the dock. He saw two long snouts. The enforcers had come to get him, Big Croc and Little Croc.

"I done wrong, Luther, trying to poison the swamp to kill that old tree. I pulled you into this mess! I'm sorry!"

Lottie buzzed by for a quick poke at Bubba. She got too close, though, and Bubba caught her. He held her lightly and then shoved her in Luther's direction.

"I'm sorry. Howa about a peace offering?" Bubba asked.

Luther's tongue shot out and caught Lottie, pulling her into his mouth.

"Don't I get no thank you?" Bubba asked.

"Ribbett!" Luther croaked as Big Croc's jaws closed around Luther, and Bubba walked home...this time.

17

GATOR CHOW

by
Scott Amis

Harold looked up at the sky. A late evening storm was brewing. His partner Eric checked the GPS tracker, tapped the airboat pilot, and pointed. "That's it, Johnny." Johnny throttled back, and the boat glided to a stop at a tiny island nearly hidden by tall swamp grass.

"Ready, Hal?" Eric said.

"Yeah. Let's go."

"Good hunting, guys," Johnny said. "I need to get back before the weather turns bad."

Harold and Eric climbed out of the boat. Harold slapped Johnny's back. "Drive careful." Johnny nodded and throttled up. The boat moved away slowly and quietly.

"Glad you could come on short notice, Hal. HQ would have sent that dork Johnson."

"I never turn down a good paying job, but I hardly had time to gather my gear. I hope you're well briefed."

"I'm up on it. There's a shallow-water trail that connects the islands. I'll lead." Both men pulled on night vision headsets, and Harold followed Eric through calf-deep water.

At the next island, Eric halted. "You armed up?"

"Better believe it." Harold pulled his Colt 1911 from beneath his poncho.

"Good that you put on the suppressor. Lotsa big gators in this area. We can't alert our man if we have to shoot a couple." They moved in single file to the next island. Eric checked his GPS again. "This is it. Let's go in slow."

Harold spotted a shack in the thick growth of maple trees ahead. The glow of a dim lamp lit the windows. "You look around back and I'll check the view inside," Eric said. They split and crept forward. Harold saw only a generator and a boatshed at the water's edge. Rain blew in gusting sheets as he met Eric at the far end. Eric grinned and held up a tranquilizer-dart pistol. "Nailed him through an open window. We'll secure him and wait this storm out. Johnny can't make it back till morning."

Inside the shack, Eric dragged the unconscious prisoner face-down to a stout metal pipe and cuffed his hands around it. He picked up a half-empty bottle of bourbon and poured a stiff drink. "Want some?" Harold poured himself a short one. Eric raised his glass.

"Hal, you never were much of a drinker, even when those rebels in Afghanistan were shooting at us." Eric raised his glass. "No matter. Here's to another mission accomplished. Those idiot feds wouldn't know what to do without guys like us." They clinked glasses. Eric emptied his and settled down on the prisoner's rumpled bed. He fell asleep shortly and snored.

Harold took a chair and sipped his bourbon. The prisoner groaned and rolled over. Harold's heart froze.

"Brent?"

"Yep, Hal. Your little brother Brent."

Harold downed his drink. "Jeez. The police images looked like you, but I couldn't believe it."

"I guess you and your buddy are bringing me in."

"We are."

"I'll get the needle for sure. You want that to happen to your own brother?"

"You're a dirtbag serial killer, and I have my duty."

"Yeah, I suppose so."

Both were silent for a minute, then Brent spoke. "Open the laptop on the counter and click on the financial website icon. The password and user ID are on the bottom."

Harold opened the website. "Where did you get four million bucks?"

"Online identity theft. I'm an expert."

"What were you going to do with it?"

"Get away while the getting was good."

"You're too hot to show your face."

"Got a better idea, smart boy?"

"Yeah, I do." Harold drew his pistol and shot Eric in the heart. Brent stared openmouthed at his brother.

"I was in Army Special Ops and know all the tricks of the trade," Harold said, "how to get fake IDs and passports and get your appearance changed."

"You're going to help me get away, and we split the money?"

"That's the plan, and we've got to be fast."

Brent eased his airboat out of the shed. Harold sat over Eric's naked body and tied concrete blocks to the ankles. "There's ten foot waters a mile ahead," Brent said. "Drop him over, and the gators will eat him up."

Brent slowed the boat to a stop. Harold looked at Eric. "Buddy, we did two tours together and came home to tell about it. I never dreamed I'd be making you into gator chow." The brothers heaved the body over the side and Brent throttled the boat into the darkness ahead.

18

RISING

FROM THE WATERS

by
Andy Lake

In the year of Our Lord 1662, it is hard to believe how much the land we see has changed since the Fens were drained and put to work. In the days of King William, the land was all marshes and swamps from Boston to Cambridge. The Isle of Ely could only be reached by boat or by wading chest deep in the murkiest water ever to drown a soul.

Evil roamed those desolate lands. Ravaged by Vikings, Danes, and then the Normans, it was the darkest of dark lands, a home to cutthroats, thieves, and fugitives. How many are the bones that lie beneath our feet? How many the restless souls?

And it is said that on a moonlit night, with chilled winds blowing the reeds, weird beings would rise from the swamp. Some say they were half frog, half men, and summoned by spells in secret ceremonies where witches danced while fallen monks chanted in demonic tongues.

In those days a Saxon woman, Aefra by name, left her home in Crowland and took the same path on the same night each year. She traveled past the Abbey, through the woods, and into the swamps beyond.

Ten years before the men had raided her village leaving her for dead beside the body of her husband. They took her fair Wilona, her only child. They ravaged village after village, dragging out many into the swamplands to do with them what cruel men did in lawless times. Aefra searched high and low until one day she found some of her daughter's blood-bespattered clothing. Sure that Wilona's body lay within the swamp, she tarried many days weeping constantly. Tying a strip of Wilona's dress on the lone field maple that stood by the swamp, she marked Wilona's unholy grave.

Each year Aefra went out alone into the swamps to pray for her child by the side of the maple. Yet her suffering grew, rather than lessened, as she thought of her child's cold body lying in corruption and all alone in the swamp. Now Aefra was determined to end her suffering. She would join her daughter at the bottom of the swamp. She would cradle the head of her child who would no longer be alone.

Aefra hurried into the dark woods and hesitated. Ahead she espied a strange figure rushing clumsily through the undergrowth. An owl screeched. The hairs on her neck stood on end, but nothing could deter her. Soon she would be reunited with her child.

Reaching the edge of the swamp, she saw her maple. It was the time. She gathered stones into her bag. She would hang it around her neck and walk into the waters till they consumed her.

At that moment the waters swelled as a creature rose from the depths of the swamp. It was covered in mud. It thrashed and writhed, and uttered the vilest curses imaginable. Plunging down, it re-emerged amidst hideous cries.

Dropping the bag Aefra stood transfixed. She had never heard such suffering and anguish. It tore at her heart echoing the pain in her own soul. Whether it was man or beast or demon, she was drawn inexorably toward it.

As rain lashed down she plunged into the swamp toward the creature. At her touch it spun round with eyes that witnessed great affliction and despair. Tears were streaking the mud on his cheeks. Wordlessly she put her arm around him, supported his abject body, and they stumbled to the edge.

He lay there shaking his head and choking all the while. She wiped mud from his eyes, from his nose, and from his lips with gentle fingers. She sat beside him and felt confused. Her resolution was gone.

At last the man—for man it was—told her of his grief. He described how his wife and child were taken while he was away fighting the Normans. His attempt to drown himself failed on this desperate anniversary night.

As the pouring rain washed the stinking mud from her face bit by bit, Aefra knew something with certainty. Wilona and this man's son had called them to the swamp and brought them together.

This is how Aefra learned that when she walks in the valley of the shadow of death, she would fear no evil, neither from the evil men of this world nor from the phantom shapes of another. She wears a talisman around her neck. It was made by her many-times-great-grandfather. On it is written:

AMOR VINCIT OMNIA

This means *love conquers all.* Many believe it is so.

19

SWAMP CYCLES

by
Jenise Erikson

I've lived in the Louisiana swamp all my life. My great grandpa built the stilted house I live in now. He was a woodworker by trade, as is my grandpa and father. I live here with my mom and dad, my three siblings, and my paternal grandparents. We make our living off the land, finding one hundred year old Cypress trees and turning them into something sellable. It's a family business, and we all do our part. I've been raised in the business and reckon I'll stick with it.

Last Saturday old man LeBlanc and his clan pulled their pirogues to the banks of our land and stepped out with their shotguns, four in all. "Breaux! I want a word with you. Maintenant, venir ici!"

Daddy, Pappaw, and my younger brother, Rene, hauled out of the house toting their twelve gauges as well. I peeped from my Dad's shop to watch the show. "Jacques, what can I do you for? I ain't seen you down my way since last year's Fais Do-Do. I s'pect you's got a gripe wit me. Speak yor mind. What's got yor feet a tappin'?"

"Don't act like you don't know what's happenin' here Jean Breaux! We've been friends long enough. You and yours was creepin' on my property yester-hier, thievin' my logs. I seen yor son schlepping away with my barrier. You know darn well that log's been layin' there since my grandpappy 'stablished us in these parts. The log kept my banks from washin' away and made stable my dock. Now, put it back where ya found it to show what kind of man you are."

"See here, Jacques LeBlanc. You know what's in the water is fair game. We took her legal. Don't be spoutin' 'bout it was yors when I found her fifty feet from yor banks. Now get outta here with la famille for somebody gets hurt."

"I 'spect you best give me the log now 'fore I have to take the law into my own hands."

"Too late for that Jacques. I done cut her up."

Jacques and his boys started to lift their weapons, but Errol and Francois came up from near the pirogues and aimed their 30-30 Winchesters at the trespassers.

Errol said, "You've overstayed your welcome, Mr. LeBlanc. It's time for you to go." Both boys clicked down the hammers on their carbines. "We'll be seein' ya or perhaps not." Errol snickered.

LeBlanc and his family members withdrew to their canoes and motored away. Daddy and the rest retired back into the house while Errol and Francois came over to the shop. They were whooping and hollering, bursting out laughing.

"We left 'em a little going away present in the pirogue," Errol said. "Wooeeey! I 'spect they'll be findin' it about right now!" Errol and Francois are bent over holding their guts and slapping their knees. "Them moccasins we found yester-heir make a mighty fine gift.

"What'd you say Lisette?" My thoughts trailed off to yesterday's event. The boys and I were hunting spotted salamanders near an abandoned houseboat deep in the swamp. An old maple gave up trying to survive in this wetland and collapsed on top of the boat. Near the roots a nest of cottonmouths had made their home. The boys snagged five big ones. They were good eatin'. They were deadly.

Lately the economy has changed my family's behavior. Furniture hasn't been selling so good, and Dad and Mom have been fighting more. The boys are totally out of control. Dad would've never taken LeBlanc's log a year ago. LeBlanc's family is good people. I thought we were supposed to be.

The boys left and I went back to work milling the new lumber from LeBlanc's old barrier. Daddy left it up to me to use the lumber as I saw fit. I took the freshly cut wood and started designing the new pieces.

A couple of days later, an article in the Daily Enterprise read in part:

Four family members die from fatal bites: While hunting gators last week in the Atchafalaya Swamp, Jacques LeBlanc and his three sons were attacked by poisonous snakes. LeBlanc's life-long friend, Jean Breaux and family, donated handmade coffins for the four victims. The destitute family has struggled financially with their cabinet business since the economic downturn.

Business is booming lately. Life on the swamp moves in cycles. Death generates vacancies and opportunities for survivors, but sometimes you've got to create your own to survive.

20

FREEDOM FLIGHT

by
Mike Boggia

Vikki slipped away from the playground tormentors. Blinded by tears, she dashed into a maple forest and stumbled down a winding trail to a swamp. She heard a school bell, signaling the end of lunch hour. She ran.

Her parents abandoned her to an orphanage where kids teased her unmercifully. Scars disfigured her face and arms. She faintly remembered a man growl, "Don't mess with fire," and she remembered the searing pain.

She wandered from the path and through the trees greening with spring. She pushed on not knowing where she was going, only that it was away from the children who bullied her.

Tears spent and body exhausted, she stopped and wiped her nose with a tiny soiled rag from her jumper's pocket. The swamp was silent, unusual for a spring afternoon. A muffled cry of fear came to her, so faint she thought her ears deceived her. It came again from her left. She carefully picked her way through the mud.

She saw the source hunched on a fallen log. It resembled a lizard charred by fire. The arrow shaped head lifted. Four liquid silver eyes with ruby slit pupils scrutinized her. He snorted. His black scarred skin turned blood red. His stubby spiny tail twitched, and his muscles tightened preparing to leap. He opened his mouth revealing a black lining, triple tongues, and sharp green fangs.

A piercing wail shook leaflets on the maples. Vikki held her ears. They stared at each other. The beast slowly relaxed and sank back on the log. His head swiveled and his slit nostrils flared wide. Orange frills rose from within undulating in the air.

Satisfied with the results of the examination, he slumped back on the log clinging tightly to the wood with sturdy clawed feet and with supple fore and rear legs.

The sniveling sound began again. Her instincts warned her to flee, yet the pitiful sounds from the creature kept her rooted.

She drew a deep breath. "Are you lost?" Not that she expected an answer. "My name is Vikki. What's yours?" The head swiveled toward her. "I'll call you Orphie, okay?"

Orphie slowly rose from the trunk, eased his three-foot long body to the ground, and inched toward her. He stopped at arm's length and settled on his haunches. Nostrils flared scenting the air. He sank to his belly and slithered to her feet. Vikki studied the creature's rough alligator-like skin. She crouched and gently touched his head. Orphie shuddered and sprang to his feet. At the same moment, she jumped back. He bounced up and down on his front feet uttering gargling sounds.

Vikki giggled at his antics. "We scared each other, didn't we?"

Orphie crawled up to her and nudged her leg with his snout. She petted him initiating more puppyish antics. His pupils sparked electric blue light. He sat up on his hind legs and gently touched her arm with his rough clawed hands. The gargle continued soft and melodious. He gingerly touched her cheek and cooed.

Vikki unburdened herself as they walked between skunk cabbages at the edge of the swamp. Orphie kept pace. He replied with a gargle and a coo.

The forest abruptly shook from a harsh scream. The force knocked Vikki on her bottom. Orphie reared and shrieked in reply.

Something large crashed through the forest and a seven-foot version of Orphie appeared. It must be his mother. She stopped. A freight train rumbled from her throat and glared at Vikki. Orphie dropped to all four and raced to her. They turned and quickly disappeared between the trees.

"Wait." Vikki's outstretched arms reached for Orphie. Alone. Tears flowed. She sank down on the leaves and wished she could die.

Orphie stopped short of the entrance to the shimmering triangular spacecraft and peered up at his mother.

She scanned his mind and nodded.

The next thing Vikki knew, she found herself in a vehicle of rainbow hues sitting beside Orphie. His foreleg was around her shoulders. She felt love, warmth, and happiness oozing from this strange creature and his mother. It was more love than she dared to dream or thought existed. In time she understood their language and realized she was Orphie's pet, but it didn't matter. A beloved pet is better than being a shunned hated human.

CHAPTER 2

CLIMATE CHANGE

21

THE STORM GODDESS

by
Arlene Lagos

Another restless night filled with brutal nightmares has woken me. Always dreaming the same dream, it starts with me standing on top of a mountain. The wind is blowing brutally almost knocking me over. There is a clock ticking in the distance, like a countdown, and I am holding a piece of paper and reciting a spell. The weather is volatile unlike anything I have ever seen. The earth shakes beneath me. The sun seems to be getting closer to the earth, burning my back by the second. I finish the spell and it makes it all stop. Then I am ripped out of my bed and awake again.

Troubled by these nightmares, I go for a walk to the local bookstore. As I peruse the aisles looking for another trashy romance novel to cuddle up to, I feel the earth begin to shake beneath my feet. This is odd to me, for earthquakes are very rare in New England. As I brace myself between the two shelves, a book falls off one of them and opens up at my feet. I've seen this book before. It's old and dusty with yellowed paper. Finally, the ground stops shaking.

I pick up the book and sit down in a nearby chair. At first glance it looks like a book of recipes, and then I realize that it is a book of spells. How did this end up in the romance section? I pour through the pages, all the while feeling like someone is staring at me. I continue to browse the pages when I hear chatter growing louder and I turn my attention to the commotion.

Droves of patrons were staring out the window in awe. It was…snowing! Which is not all that strange for New England, except that it's the middle of July!

This felt familiar. I've…dreamt this.

As I recall the recent events, I notice a man staring at me again. I walk up to him and ask him what's going on, but he seems unable to speak. The snow is coming down harder outside, and the people in the store begin to panic. Quickly he grabs the book from my hands, flips through it, and rips out one of the spells. He turns it over and writes something on the back of it, hands it to me, and runs off.

When I flip it back over, the name of the spell is called *The Storm Goddess*. On the back of the spell he wrote four words:

IT'S NOT A DREAM

The sound of my alarm startles me, and I sit up in my bed covered in sweat. Great, now I am dreaming about dreaming. I lean over, grab the glass of water by my bed, and take a sip. When I put it back down, I notice a piece of paper on the floor. It's yellowed and crumbled, and I recognize it instantly.

As soon as I pick it up, I feel a rumbling beneath my feet—another earthquake. Then the sky goes dark outside, and the snow starts again. I look at the clock and it is counting down. Whatever I am supposed to do, I only have fifteen minutes left. I quickly get dressed, grab my purse and keys, and fling open the door only to find that same man standing in front of me.

Behind him was no longer my hallway, but a doorway to another part of the world. I remember this from my dream. He put out his hand, but I hesitated to take it. He looked at me and I could hear him speaking to me with his thoughts. He said, "Our storm Goddess is dead. You are her predecessor. We need your help to keep the balance, or your planet will die."

I look back at the clock. Twelve minutes. I look back at the man. "Are we going to the mountain?" I ask.

The man smiles and nods in relief. He holds out his hand again, and I hold out mine. Together we walk through the doorway towards the mountain to save the world…with ten minutes to spare.

CARBON NEUTRAL

by
Douglas G. Clarke

Monday—Carbon Futures $195/ton

Jill and John were arguing. In three days, if they hadn't made a decision, it would be made for them with the coming of M3724.

"If we get rid of our cars and get a new electric one, I'll be able to commute to the city and take that new job. We can sell the extra credits and you won't have to work," said John.

"If we get rid of both cars and just ride our bicycles we can afford to have a child. Don't you want a baby?" asked Jill, with a plea in her voice. "And I don't mind working."

"Of course I do. We might be able to afford the carbon credits, but how can we afford to buy food for another mouth on what I make now? Let alone a bigger house."

Jill frowned. "But if carbon futures go up like the market is predicting, this is our last chance."

Tuesday—Carbon Futures $405/ton

The TV blared, "Scientists have raised estimates of how much carbon dioxide M3724 might leave as it passes our atmosphere to 780 million tons. On this news the market surged and trading was halted with carbon futures at a all time high."

Dr. Smith smiled at Jill and John. "It's true that once we've implanted the fetus, the government won't make you abort it, but that doesn't mean they can't make you lower your carbon footprint in other ways. If things get as bad as some of the experts are saying, you could lose your stove and even your hot water. Are you sure you want to go through with this?"

John looked at Jill and could see the answer in her eyes. "Yes, Doctor. We're sure."

Wednesday—Carbon Futures $1,329/ton

Jill and John sat on their back porch watching the evening sky. John had sold their cars and contracted with the power company to buy another megawatt of power a month from their solar array.

Jill had spent the morning at the clinic. With Dr. Smith's written orders, her frozen embryo had been implanted. In nine months she would be a mother.

"We're doing the right thing, aren't we?" asked Jill.

"From the joy I've seen in your eyes today, I know we are."

"Can you see it?" asked Jill. "The sunlight is reflecting off of it."

John looked where she was pointing. "Yep. Looks like it's moving. It's supposed to be quite a show tomorrow when it skips along the atmosphere."

They spent the next couple of hours watching the sky and talking about the future, and then went into their dark house to sleep.

Thursday—Carbon Futures $5,989/ton—market closed

The streets were filled with people all waiting to see M3724. Jill and John sat on their porch, ice tea in hand, and watched with them.

A gasp from the crowd and a thousand pointing fingers announced M3724's arrival. First a small black speck—it grew quickly—then it became red, and a tail grew behind it.

The tail abruptly disappeared. The crowd gathered and yelled in unison, "One!"

A few seconds passed. The tail grew again. Three seconds later the tail disappeared.

"Two!" the crowd erupted.

Everyone knew that the asteroid would skip two to four times, each time leaving more carbon in its wake. Everyone was hoping for just two.

When the tail appeared again the crowd moaned. The tail flared for five seconds.

It faded.

"Three," the crowd yelled only to be followed by a louder moan when the tail appeared again.

When the tail disappeared there was a less enthusiastic yell, "Four."

The crowd accepted that the worst case had occurred, and the government would mandate more carbon reductions.

When the tail appeared for a fifth time the crowd was horrified. It burned across the sky, leaving millions of tons a second of carbon dioxide behind.

Five seconds, then ten seconds passed. The tail didn't disappear. Instead it grew longer, and M3742 grew brighter. In an instance it was gone and replaced with a blinding flash.

Jill and John held hands as the sounds of the panicky crowd washed over them.

"We made the right choice," said Jill.

"Yes, we did," replied John, and he squeezed her hand gently. "I'm so glad I got to see you happy one last time."

John embraced Jill, holding her tight until the shockwave reached them, releasing them both from this world.

23

TALKING TURKEY

by
Laura Stafford

Emily picked at the green beans and pushed the mashed potatoes around on her plate, wishing she was back at the kids' table. The same discussion that had lasted for as long as she could remember revolved around the table again, and Emily was starting to get annoyed.

It always began the same. "The cost of the turkey went up this year by thirty cents a pound!" her grandmother would admonish.

"It's the stupid gas prices ..." her grandfather would mutter.

"The economy just isn't what it used to be," Emily's mother frowned.

"It's the unions," Cousin Johnny always chimed.

"It's the upper class," Aunt Vera would argue.

"It's the stupid government," said Grandpa through a mouthful of sweet potatoes.

Around and around, the plot would thicken as it

jumped from opinion to opinion, until everyone at the table was arguing about politics and the state of the world.

And this was all fine by Emily until the real bone of contention was put out on the table to chew.

"It's because the younger generation has lost their religion," said her mother, looking pointedly at Emily.

"Oh, yes," Gramma agreed. "If they believed in God and put their faith to work, there wouldn't be all that blasphemous programming on the television. Our children's morals are being corrupted every day."

"Our country is in imminent danger because we don't trust in God," says her mother, staring Emily down. "They don't even go to church anymore."

The sky is falling! The sky is falling! Emily thought, but said nothing.

Emily took a deep breath. Maybe she could slide under the table and escape to the pumpkin pie without being noticed.

"It's the stupid scientists." Her grandfather spat into his napkin. "It's ten degrees outside, but the stupid idiots are hollerin' 'bout global warming. P'shaw!"

And the sky started falling on Emily.

"It's about global temperatures, Grandpa," said Emily quietly.

"Yer a scientist. Go on and sing it, Em." Johnny pushed her.

"I'm just a student." Emily glared at him.

"How is school going this year?" Aunt Vera asked

gently.

Emily couldn't stop herself from replying honestly. "Good. I just started my paleontology class and, well…" Now that it was already out of her mouth, there was no turning back. Emily almost slapped herself in the forehead. "You know I like that stuff …"

"Ain't nobody ever going to make me believe we came from stupid apes." Grandpa coughed.

"It's ridiculous!" Emily's mother shouted now. "There is too much perfection in nature to believe that it happened by some … some random chance. God created us all the way we are, and it's the way it will be forever."

The sky crashed down.

Emily rolled her eyes.

"Don't take that tone with me!" Her mother leaned over her plate, greying hair almost touching the pool of gravy.

"It's the stupid schools," her grandfather intoned.

"Yes, if they would bring God back into the schools—"

Emily didn't let her grandmother finish. She felt the launch of a tirade boiling in the pit of her stomach. "Sometimes having dinner here gives me an ulcer!" She yelled at them, standing up from the cold turkey and warming cranberry sauce. "It's freakin' Thanksgiving for Pete's sake! Can't we just have one dinner where we don't talk about how crappy things are? Can't we just have one dinner where we go around the table like little kids and just say what we're happy about?"

She shook her head huffing, sat back down, and looked at all of them. They stared back silently. Her mother sighed. Gramma made a coughing noise at the back of her throat. Aunt Vera fluttered her hands, and Johnny kicked back crossing his arms with one giant guffaw.

"I'll start," offered Emily. "I'm happy that this is one more year I get to yell at you guys around the dinner table."

* * *

When she returned to school that Sunday evening, there was a note waiting for Emily in her mailbox.

It read:

Emily,

Don't forget to call your grandmother when you get in. You know how she worries. We are always happy and thankful for you and the family we cherish. We love and miss you!

Mom

24

RIDING OUT THE STORM

by
Kristen Strassel

Independence Day has always been my favorite holiday. Every year my parents brought me to the grand parade thrown by America's hometown, my hometown. It was only right that I did the same for my kids. Even if on this July fourth, snow fell gently from the sky like the glittering decent of spent fireworks.

"Mom! I don't want to go to the parade! It's freezing!" Rachel, my ten year old whined. I didn't blame her. I didn't really want to go either. I also didn't want this tradition to die just because of a little snow in July. It scared me, but I didn't want the kids to know I was concerned.

Parking was more challenging than ever. Not only was there extra traffic and many streets closed due to the parade, but plows moved piles of snow bigger than my car to the sides of the road, making some of the spots disappear. People in patriotic gear darted out from behind the drifts, forced me to slam on the breaks, and I prayed I didn't hit a patch of ice and kill someone. We headed for our traditional spot, in front of Pioppi's Package Store.

"Do you think they'll still throw candy out from the floats with all this snow?" asked five-year old Simon.

"I hope so, kiddo." Nothing dampened this kid's appetite for sugar.

A commotion broke out on the street corner. A large crowd gathered and jeered. I wasn't sure if it was safe to bring the kids towards it, but we were all too curious to walk away. None of us could believe our eyes when we saw the Reverend Paul Masterson perched high atop a snowdrift pleading with God to save all of our souls. *The end was near*, he insisted. The kids looked to me wide eyed for an explanation. I had none. I pulled them close to me as we attempted to circumvent the mob. For the first time I truly feared for our safety.

Many of the Reverend's prophets had turned out in support of his message. They forced pamphlets upon everyone who passed by. The snowy ground was littered with them. I didn't take one, and I wouldn't let the kids take them either. I didn't want to know what doomsday prophecy it contained.

We reached our usual spot and greeted our friends. The crowd was abuzz with the word of the Reverend. He'd pulled some crazy stunts in the past, but to come here, to Plymouth, and proclaim the end of the world?

The parade seemed more crowded than usual this year, or maybe we all just huddled together for warmth.

Street peddlers sold neon jewelry and hot cocoa. I bought bright necklaces and a cup of hot chocolate for the kids to enjoy while we waited for the festivities to begin.

The beat of the marching band breaking through the slush signaled the beginning of the parade. The majestic floats passed by with a bit more care than prior years, but they were no less impressive. To Simon's delight, they still threw candy to the kids in the crowd. Besides my wet feet freezing through my boots, it was Independence Day tradition at its finest.

Off in the distance, a cannon cracked. That seemed odd. The town never did the Twenty One Gun Salute until nightfall for the fireworks. The adults all seemed to know something was off, looking around to one another to find the source of the explosion.

None of us thought to look up until someone screamed.

"Run! Oh my God!" The crowd erupted into chaos. Revelers mixed with marching bands and town selectmen in the middle of the street. I grabbed the kids and ran, barely looking back to see Benny's Department Store as it erupted into flames.

"Meteors! They're coming from everywhere!"

"Oh my God! The sky is falling!"

Is this what the Reverend tried to warn us about?

Instinctively I led the kids back towards the car, but would that be safe? Would anything be safe again? I led them back into the minivan, now covered with a fresh layer of snow, and climbed in the backseat with them, hoping we could ride out the storm.

BAD RAIN

by
Jot Russell

On the day I was born, there was what the Philippine people call a *bad rain*. Try to consider a month-long monsoon. Now consider that all falling in a single day. A foot of rain not spread across a vast plain, but collected into small valleys between steep mountains within a truly three-dimensional landscape.

My mother exited her seminar on climate change, surprised by the sudden storm and her broken water from my warm wet chamber. Soaking wet but thankful for the rainy camouflage of her condition, my mother hailed a cab to the nearest hospital. The rain fell hard and obscured her view outside as the car raced through. Cold and wet she pulled out the card from my father and read it once more.

I love you

The note gave her the warmth and confidence she

needed.

A taxi stopped at a two-story clinic that seemed little more than an oversized home. It was dry within, aside from the slippery floor that my mother shuffled across while holding her belly. With one look the wise doctor could tell my arrival was imminent. He took my mother's arm and led us over to a room on the first floor. It had blue wallpaper decorated with desert recipes, an adjustable bed, yellow curtains, a green oxygen tank with an attached mask, and various tools.

My mother moaned before making it to the bed that the doctor directed her towards. Once there the pains continued and quickly grew in frequency. Outside the rain came down even heavier, finding its path to coalesce with a trillion other drops into an already overburdened aquifer.

Slowly I slid down and pushed myself to the edge of the channel. The doctor confirmed, "I see the head."

Off in the distance, the small village dam succumbed to the overflow of water around its foundation. The landslide unleashed a wall of mud and water that drew its sights on the town as I was preparing to draw my first sights on the world.

My mother pushed and screamed from the pains of labor, drowning out the unnatural rumble that loomed in the distance. As I made my way out and into the hands of the doctor, the cold air triggered my own cries of protest. He quickly cleaned me up and handed me to my mom. Once again we were together providing each other warmth and calm.

In the room's silence, the outside ruckus became suddenly apparent. The doctor gave a confused expression and quickly rushed toward the first story window. Just then the wave crashed through washing him out to the hall and down towards the staircase.

The cement building held, but the water started to fill the room, pushing my mother's bed against one of the support beams. She held me as the cold turbulent water raised higher. Using what might be her last breath, my mother held me up as the water rose toward the ceiling. Instead of having me cough in dirty water, she covered my mouth and we floated toward the green tank. Holding me in her grasp, we drifted underwater toward the wall next to the supplies.

She clung to the oxygen tank and managed to turn on the handle. My mother and I took turns using the mask.

Five seconds passed. Ten. Twenty.

The current through the room slowed, but the first level of the building remained full of water. Stricken with panic and grief, my mother strained to see any exit from this watery grave. With a loss of hope, my mother's will gave way to the burning in her lungs. She opened her mouth but drew in a watery breath.

Once the initial flow from the dam passed, the water level dropped and quickly drained from the building. The doctor had held onto the staircase railing and managed to pull himself up to the second level. With the receding water, he pushed his way back down the stairs and into our room. There in the corner, he saw us still clenching the oxygen bottle, sharing breaths from the attached mask.

I love when my mother tells me that story. Did I mention my sister was born on the moon?

26

THE AL GORE RHYTHM

OF

CLIMATE CHANGE

by
Richard Bunning

Climate change is a short story. It is a story as short as Al Gore's 64 years, in the year of 2012, although of course it starts way back, well before the first little critters appeared in the muddy wet coastal areas of planet Earth. These microbial thingies happened to be flapping away very close to where Washington, DC stands today. Note that it is only the very last bit of change that is a top concern.

To study climate change we need some climate rules. The first important one is just, *An Inconvenient Truth*, namely that constant change makes planning ahead really difficult. The second rule is, of course, that climate constantly changes. Exactly the same climate is sure to exist all the time in the infinity of space. Well, how can there be infinity without nauseous repetition? It stands to reason doesn't it! As any old Pre-Cambrian fossil will tell you, if it could, "We really just have very long weather. I've seen it all before."

So are we in a period that is really just a bit of unseasonal weather, which very old things like Al Gore have been through before, but can't always remember, or a period of unique change. The political climate idea of Al's is not strictly helpful. After all what exactly does *just look at my records* mean? Whose are we to choose, his records, his father's, the potpourri of dynasties like the Kennedys? JFK possibly did more to stop climate change than just about anyone, when he helped avoid meltdown from the Cuban Missile Crisis. Even the hard work of Al has done little in comparison.

This powerful climatic story needed a focus, a test; proof would help. Easy, all that was needed was for me to go back in time, and have a good look at what the weather was like historically. Being a short story I had to be targeted. I decided to simply nip back to the 31st of March 1948, and have a look. That was the day on which perhaps the best-known political climate man of this age was born. Yes, that is right, one Albert Arnold Gore.

I purposely stepped back 64 years from the present on the 31st of March 2012. This decision was, as it happened, entirely consistent with mathematics. You see, 64 is the smallest number exactly divisible by seven, which just happens to be the number of types of fundamental catastrophes in mathematics, the foundation-stone of all sciences. One of the most interesting of these is the Butterfly catastrophe.

A Butterfly Effect, which is politically related in the strangest of ways, concerns a certain *Blue* that on the 31st of March, 1948, was sitting on the windowsill of Pauline LaFon Gore's bedroom. The maid opened the window to let it out, and so changed not just the life of this butterfly, but the climate as we know it. You see that butterfly's flapping wings disturbed the air and set in store a weather pattern from which the political climate of the United States of America might never recover.

If the butterfly could have restrained its fluttering, the climate may have been left more stable. This wasn't to be. The poor thing got stuck on a couple of old Bush(s), the second by the narrowest of hanging chad margins, so eventually ensuring that Al Gore would never have the political wind he really needed.

So what did this algorithmic flight of the butterfly do to the breeze that so dramatically change the climate? Well, the flapping set in motion the weather that started the Great Spring Snow Melt Flooding Disaster. This terrible flooding lasted for over 45 soggy days. Initially warm too early, the Spring of 1948 turned into a wet and cold old time.

I was pleased to get out of the wet, back to the then present, I can tell you. What do you think I noticed when I got home? Well, don't you know it? March 2012 was the warmest, and one of the driest, March's on record in Washington, ever. Well, ever might be overdoing it. It got quite hot on Earth before the top of hell froze over, giving us the crusty Earth.

So there you have it, a short story that demonstrates, once and for all, that Al Gore really is an outstanding harbinger of climate change, even if not of political fortune. We should all really, really listen!

27

SYSA'S STAR

by
Alli Vaughan

Wizard Ryclaw's steed flung clumps of dirt wildly about in the air as it raced through the thicket. Ryclaw's elf apprentice, Sysa, trailed behind her on a heavy-hoofed pony. The little elf had been ripped away before from her comforting night of rest by the tall wizard's desperate shouts and hasty exit hours. But this time her slight back ached during the journey.

She sputtered after inhaling a cloud of dust kicked up by reckless hooves. Her eyes traced the human wizard's form pulling further and further ahead. "Ryclaw, Mr. Wizard, you're going too fast! My pony can't keep up." Her voice sounded meek above the backbreaking speed and a rush of the wind.

"Sysa, we've no time. We must catch the falling star."

"But ... why, Mr. Ryclaw?" Her innocent eyes shone brightly in the night. She gripped her pony's saddle wishing she were snuggled in front of the fire pit.

"The letter! Now faster, elf!"

"Yes, Mr. Ryclaw."

They raced toward the crest of a valley until her limbs ached. Sysa felt her knees jerk as her pony stopped suddenly. Wizard Ryclaw jumped off his horse and wrung his hands in worry as his horse pawed the soft earth. "No, it's going to fall before we make it."

"Why is that?" Sysa yawned, wishing for her soft feather bed.

"Sysa, the king needs that star. Without it, the kingdom's lost."

"Oh, is that what the note was about, Mr. Ryclaw, wizard, sir?"

"Yes, he charged me to catch a falling star, or war will break out."

"War?" Sysa's eyes widened.

"Yes, the two lands of flame and shard have warred for years, and a hasty alliance hangs in the balance."

"What alliance?" she asked.

"The Flame King plans to wed the Ice Queen, but she's as cold as her namesake and will not accept the marriage of alliance unless he can produce a rare gem for a wedding band."

"The star?" Sysa asked. Understanding fluttered onto her gentle face like a butterfly.

"Yes, Sysa. And we are not the only ones who seek it. The queen's own brother is after the star as well. He and his men plan to prevent the alliance by destroying the gem, and they will kill us if they can."

"Well, we better hurry, Mr. Wizard, sir."

"Yes, but I am afraid we are too late."

"Not for an elf," Sysa laughed. She wiggled her pink nose. Off they flew—mounts and all—toward the falling star.

Ryclaw laughed, surprised at the skill of his young apprentice.

She set them down. Her magic was spent, and she shot him a wide grin.

"Sysa, you did well," he whispered. "Now rest. I will do the rest." He patted her on the head in thanks and stared up at the trail of the falling star. Sysa smiled, for the star would fall near them, and Ryclaw would recover it.

Sysa called out suddenly in an emotionally choked voice. "Mr. Wizard, sir!"

"What, Sysa?"

"Men from the land of shard are coming!" She pointed as a several men riding giant lizards thundered toward them.

"The star, confound it." It was falling and they would not reach it before the men were upon them.

"What will you do?" Sysa asked in fear.

"Grab the pony and my horse and flee!"

"Mr. Ryclaw!"

"Do it!" he shouted.

The shard lizards and the vicious men riding them licked their lips in anticipation, murderous looks on their faces. Sysa could feel their eyes on her back as she raced away. She stopped one hundred feet away and turned to watch her teacher. "Oh, Mr. Wizard, please be careful." A tear trickled down her soft cheek.

The star drew close the earth, bursting in brilliant color as it neared its collision. The brightness blinded her, and she could only imagine the reptiles and malicious humans closing in on Ryclaw.

She knew he would want her to flee—especially with her magic spent—but her small feet planted in the ground like thick roots. "I will," Sysa whispered to herself, balling her tiny fists. Without another thought, she grabbed the reins of her pony and charged toward the light of the star. Blasts and firelight were the last things her eyes caught before closing, but she felt the warmth of Ryclaw's arms about her as he carried her away from the battle.

"You did it, Sysa and we're saved because of you, you dear elf." Ryclaw's tears glimmered in his eyes. Sysa smiled back warmly, and her eyes closed as a smile spread over her soft cheeks.

28

NATURE AND THE GIANTS

by
Harry Alexiou

Walter Mosley sat forward and stared disbelievingly at a note that landed on his desk. It seemed as though a new age of renewable energy attracted dirty interests from the scum of the underworld.

One hundred million dollars was a lot of money. Where would they get it within twenty-four hours? Not getting it wasn't really an option.

As Chief Scientist on the project, he was well aware of the threat of industrial sabotage, and he knew that they were powerless to stop a concerted effort. Looking at the letter, he could tell the groundwork may have already been prepared. The thought that he may be sitting on a time bomb sent shivers down his spine as he moved to grab the inter-office communicator.

The scientist held the devise to his cheek for a moment as he looked up to the large *old world* clock ticking above his office door. The minute hand clunked loudly and deliberately past each second, and it seemed to slow as he watched. What he wouldn't give to slow down time today. He called Freddy Jackson at security. "Freddy? Walter. Don't move. I'm coming over."

"Sure, but what—?" Freddy was all the way over in C-Wing, and it was a good 500-yard dash across the plant.

Mosley was a fit fifty and he picked up the pace. Fellow workers were greeted with a short 'Hi' as the scientist rushed by them. A whirlwind of a man on a life or death mission, he attracted their stares when they inquired the location of the fire.

The scientist checked his watch. The timer showed '23:48:23.' *How did I lose twelve minutes already?* He cursed the numbers and forged ahead. His breath was loud, and his footsteps louder as he reached his destination. Mosley thrust the letter forward into the security chief's chest and checked his watch again, '23:45:33.'

Freddy looked derisively at the scientist. "How do they expect to blow up the lithium power banks. This is a joke Mosley. This place is like Fort Knox."

"I know what this is," Mosley said, suddenly going off on a tangent. "This is the way the oil giants will stop our work. They fear for the future of their fossil fuel business."

"Come again?" Freddy asked.

"Think about it! Our vast banks of super efficient photo-voltaic panels have them shaking in their boots. The ground breaking processes which we have pioneered and our attempts to reverse climate change will eventually kill their business."

"You mean this?" Freddy held up the letter. "This is just a smoke screen?"

"Of course, it all makes sense now. They know that we can't get the money in twenty four hours so they'll blow it all sky high anyway and blame the terrorists." Mosley flicked his wrist and checked his watch again. "Come on. We have to get down to subterranean level one. Get your team together."

The assembled team was updated and split into pairs. As Mosley watched them spread out, he looked at his watch, '22:57:23'. They had to find it. He was sure they would find it.

Time had flown too fast. The countdown timer on his wrist read '01:52:04' and still they had nothing. They were exhausted, and Mosley feared the worst. The bank transfer would not be made. No call came, and no contact details were provided. The timer continued the relentless countdown, '01:51:45'. The order to evacuate was given.

The pain of admitting defeat to a group of power hungry, narrowed minded individuals was evident in Mosley's expression.

In the busy control room, Archie had been given the order to shut down the power-grid and prepare for the evacuation. He checked his own timer; 00:42:52. Sabotage was not really Arnie's thing but the offer of a considerable 'early retirement fund' had been too good to pass up. Arnie was the last man in the room and checked all around before initiating the overload sequence for the vast banks of batteries. As soon as it was done, he evacuated. No point hanging around to watch the fireworks.

The state-of-the-art plant, a model for future generations, was eerily empty when it happened. Archie's timer showed '00:00:00' as the ground-shaking explosion sent the fireball roaring skyward. It could be heard fifty miles away.

The resulting mushroom cloud was a sight to behold for the cartel of oil giants as they watched, smiling from the tallest building in the city.

TIME CAPSULE A.R.C.

by
Oliver Dolan

It was a sunny Saturday afternoon in May, and our dog Cassidy was digging in the backyard. She began barking and glancing my way, so naturally I came to her side to see what she had found. I looked down into the hole and saw her paw sliding on a gold shoebox-shaped chest. I removed from the ground what I later found out was a time capsule.

I opened the capsule to find only an envelope and a silver pen engraved with the initials A.R.C. Inside the envelope, a letter was sealed with a wax emblem with the same initials carved in. I meticulously opened the letter and could immediately tell it was not from our time.

Letter from Andrew Raymond Cravens, Chemist
1929

By the time this letter is discovered, it might be too

late. I have spent my entire life analyzing the many ways in which we damage our environment and the beautiful world we have been blessed with. We send dangerous toxins—billowing black clouds—into the sky for temporary gains without assessing the damage they could have on the lives of those who will follow us.

It is my hypothesis, after the staggering upward trend of pollution in this country and all over the world, that Mother Nature will unleash her inner beast through a series of disasters, including hurricanes, tsunamis, blizzards, tornados, and the like.

Coastlines will erode, trees will be torn from their soil, and many shelters will be destroyed. These events will most likely commence at the beginning of the twenty-first century, followed by the storm of all storms a decade or two later. Just when officials will begin to think that they have seen it all, this storm will come and cause the greatest devastation the world has ever seen. There shall be no warning. No man will be able to predict the destruction that this storm will cause.

I hope that the person who finds this letter will foster positive and permanent change around the planet, forever shifting the way humans take care of the natural world. Such a shift may convince Mother Nature to spare the world of catastrophe.

Andrew Raymond Cravens, Chemist

I was just a boy that day that I found Cravens' letter.

Cassidy has since passed away, and I have spent every waking moment studying the environment and assessing the damage we inflict on our planet.

When the century turned, I was finishing up school. After my graduation, the events that transpired eerily resembled the words in Cravens' letter. From the tsunami in Sri Lanka to Hurricane Katrina in the United States and to the earthquake in Japan, the frequency of natural disasters was increasing at an alarming rate. It appeared as though his prediction was right on track.

I've joined climate change groups and have teamed up with like-minded scientists. We've rallied and protested all around the world, but little progress has been made. Our ideas have been pushed away, time and time again, by political ideals and greed.

So it is now a race against time, and I feel the weight of the world on my shoulders. Questions race through my mind every day, and my dreams are haunted by horrific thoughts of people and animals being blown away, oceans swallowing towns, and the world as we know it slipping from our grasp. But my fight will not stop. Cravens wanted someone to find his letter. He wanted someone to be the last ray of hope, and someone on a mission to save our planet.

I turn on the weather channel and listen intently to the forecasting of *the storm of a lifetime*. Cravens said that the knockout punch would be dealt with no notice, but I'm still on guard.

I zip up my jacket and step out into my backyard. I

look towards the gloomy gray sky as the first raindrop hits the tip of my nose, and the increasingly strong gusts sway my body from side to side. I reach into my pockets and grip the silver pen with my right hand and the letter with my left, praying, wishing, and hoping that I still have more time.

TORNADO PAPARAZZI

by
H. M. Schuldt

A particular farmhouse had no one to save it from a twisting disaster. There it stood, an old gloomy house on the other side of a broken down fence, exposed to a roaring giant. At the edge of a small meadow, a lonely driveway led up to Sandy Cut Road near Oklahoma City.

Plowing down a country road, two vehicles, a Tornado F5 Van and a Tornado F5 Truck, raced against time to save whoever might be stuck inside. Both vehicles were armored with steel plates and bullet resistant windows. They drove down a long gravel driveway. Ace noticed rocks and tree branches flying through loud thick air like bullets and daggers. A chair on the front porch slid across the surface, slamming against the rail.

"Four bodies inside. One adult. Three kids," John said. He was a Windman Commander who sat behind a steering wheel and peered into a control panel. His mind and communication were full of quick wisdom, being able to locate those in danger. He viewed the weather screen. It provided important information designed for perilous times such as this one. A weather message only becomes valuable to the person who knows what to do with it.

THREE MINUTES UNTIL IMPACT

"Eighty miles an hour. You have three minutes! Go! Go!" John called out.

John's team was ready, fully loaded with knowledge and adrenaline. Four Windmen stepped into a strong wind as the truck door was forced to slam shut. The men in uniform shielded themselves from flying twigs and dirt. But far more alarming was a large tree branch that broke free, banging into the side of the truck. Tops and Hunter made their way toward the back door while Ace and Champ ran to the front.

Ace reached for the door handle. It was unlocked. A terrible moaning wind forced the door wide open.

"Hello! Anyone?" Ace pushed the front door shut and immediately looked for the basement.

"Hello! Rescue!" Champ called out.

Ace opened the basement door.

A woman's voice spoke from down below. "Hello?"

Four Windmen skipped down the steps three at a time.

"You have less than two minutes to get out!" Ace shouted. "It's headed right for your house!"

Champ saw a mother remaining strong for her three daughters. The loud sound had arrived so quickly. Earlier that day, the youngest child, Carla, had been happily playing pretend with her teddy bear.

"We can get you in the van. Let's go! Let's go!" Ace yelled.

The woman shook her head no. "I can't leave my house."

"You have to. It's going to take your house. If you stay, it will take you too." Ace motioned for them to move it. He reached out his hand insistently toward the obstinate woman.

The mother trembled, but with an effort she pulled herself together and began the trek upstairs after her children.

Champ led the way with three young girls following. They ran toward the front door.

Suddenly the walls rattled.

With a loud engine sound, the house began to shake. They felt a powerful rumble pressing against the backside of the house. *Crash!* A window broke into a thousand pieces.

Carla, the mother's youngest daughter, startled everyone with a scream. She cried out in fear. "Mommy!"

Champ picked her up since the wind was too strong for her. His voice was firm. "We will carry you to the van."

The mother was flooded with emotion, ignoring her family photo near the front door. She began to feel freedom in leaving her house behind, the place where she fought with her husband for years. She had given up on his callous lifestyle. She had felt trapped with his rude behavior, and believed that her life would never get better. He had refused to do any work around the house. It was her bitterness that had ruined her own marriage even though her husband had fought many demons. He believed his duty was to change his wife. She complained that he never helped with laundry and that he never helped with anything. The marriage was a downward spiral headed for destruction unless a major change happened in their life. A cheerful family photo fell to the floor and cracked.

"Mam, you have to be strong." Ace looked directly into her eyes.

A rushing wind pushed heavy against the porch. The sound was like a roaring jet engine. A third vehicle slowly pulled to the edge of the driveway—Tom's El Camino—a storm chaser. Tom and his brother were looking for the thrill of stalking a twister to take photos.

Holding onto the railing for balance, four Windmen stepped down to the ground. Another Windman, Rocket, was waiting in the van to help rescue citizens from danger. He had parked the van in the lawn right next to the porch.

A sudden gust of wind knocked the mother down to the ground.

Young Carla called out in love and worry for her mother. "Mommy!"

Champ held her tight. He quickly jumped into the back of the van with Carla while she was struggling against him. She wanted to break free into the terrible wind to save her mother.

Champ gave her instructions. "You have to stay here."

"No! Mommy fell down!" Carla desperately pushed against him, and then she bit Champ's arm. She continued to struggle and fight the Windman who was holding on to save her life.

"We will get her. You have to stay here or you will blow away in the wind," Champ spoke, ignoring the bite mark. He held her close to ensure her safety.

Carla began to pound her little fists on Champ's arm, back, and chest to save her mother. Two Windmen partners, Tops and Hunter, helped the older two girls into the van.

Outside Ace planted each foot on the ground to help the mother get up. She stumbled. Together Ace and the mother finally made it into the van. Another mean gust of wind struck, taking control of the door, slamming it shut.

"Mommy! Mommy! Are you okay?" Carla cried out in the van. Now that the door was shut, Champ let go of the young girl. Carla climbed into her mother's arms to comfort her.

A constant push on the west side of the vehicle eventually lifted two tires off the ground. It landed with a heavy bounce.

"My Teddy!" Carla reached toward the door suddenly realizing she had left her special teddy behind. It had been her lovey, the only one she looked to for comfort. She tried to get out again by moving toward the back door. Ace stopped her.

"Carla, Teddy is so old, he's falling apart," the mother scolded. "Carla, No!"

"I'm sorry, miss, no one can get out. We cannot go back," Ace said.

Tears began to fall down Carla's cheeks. She couldn't leave her Teddy behind. The young girl cried out as she reached for her only source of comfort, her dependable white Teddy who never yelled at her. "My Teddy!"

"One minute until impact! We gotta go!" Rocket called out.

Champ took the young girl in his arms again. This time she did not protest. He held her close as she sunk into his comfort.

"You're safe with us. It's not safe out there right now. It's more important you have each other," Champ said.

Three vehicles sped down a country road away from the terrible destruction of harsh swirling wind. Without warning a washing machine fell from the sky and landed right in front of the El Camino, smack in the middle of the road.

Like a kid in a candy shop, Tom swerved his El Camino around the machine just in time. He felt a thrill from being near a twister and joked wildly. "No one's doing laundry today!"

His brother also lived on the edge and took a quick photo of the washer.

John responded by swerving his truck around the beat up machine. "Looks like a washer went through hell and back."

Ace spoke as the van passed by. "Don't look back, miss."

A day later when the mother returned to her old house, she found a pile of rubble. She noticed several people taking photos. There standing in her yard was a white bathtub. Inside she found Teddy happily taking his bath. She reached out and picked him up. "Bathtime's over, Teddy. You really oughta stay with Carla."

She gave Teddy a hug when someone from the street caught the moment with a camera. Click.

31

THE PHYTOPLANKTON CARBON TRAP

by
Randy Dutton

"The aquarium's bright green ... that's not supposed to happen." Trevor muttered to himself as he clicked on the laboratory lights. His pulse raced as he quickly walked along the bank of glass tanks. Each was a similar color. That meant the carbon dioxide reduction project had worked—too well.

Flipping his cell phone open, he speed-dialed his boss. A brief recording indicated unavailability.

"Dr. Thames, this is Trevor, we've got a problem. I started an experiment Friday before I closed the research lab for the weekend. I came in early before we started our field test. I'll email a report to you and Dr. Johansson." His hand was shaking as he closed his phone.

Trevor sat down and turned on his computer. He sipped his Starbucks coffee out of habit—not for the need of stimulation—not this morning. It was 5 a.m. His nerves already were in overdrive as his fingers tapped out the short report.

Confidential:
Phytoplankton Test and Recommendation—
Do NOT proceed with Field Release.

His breathing was rapid and shallow as he recounted the details of each of the twenty test parameters and the outcomes. "A microliter of our genetically modified phytoplankton in twenty aquariums ... the phytoplankton population soared in nearly every test variable – pH, carbon dioxide level, light, temperature, nutrient levels, and with competing species ..."

He paused. "Why am I so nervous? The company will make a fortune off our other carbon sequestration products. It's not as if we needed this product's sales. Why worry? We've got time to downgrade this phytoplankton's abilities. The UN and various countries are paying other companies to genetically create similar species to end global warming. Because the consortia's billionaire CEO bankrolled this, we've got a head start. Nice when we can skirt the rules. He didn't even authorize this species for release."

He typed out his recommendation to cancel the field test scheduled a few hours later. Early morning light glinted off the stainless steel tank sitting on the barge. From his window Trevor observed deck hands preparing the self-propelled barge for the phytoplankton release in San Francisco Bay.

His office door swung open violently as a portly middle-aged man entered.

"Trevor, who authorized you to conduct that test? I'm the Operations Manager and every test goes through me!"

Trevor's hands started shaking again. "Dr. Thames, I, ah, figured we could use more data ... just to be sure."

"Why?"

Trevor responded nervously, "My doctorate is in invasive species propagation. I just wanted to be sure that the most recent genetic manipulation doesn't create a problem for us ... for the Earth. If you look at—"

"Who else did you send that email to?" Thames interrupted. His face was beet red.

"Just you and Dr. Johansson, the head of Snath Genetics, sir."

"Who else have you mentioned this to?"

"No one, sir."

Thames paused in thought. "Okay, here's what you do. Delete every copy of your report and that email. Don't talk to anyone about your test or the release!"

Trevor watched as his boss started to walk out of the office and into the lab.

Thames picked up a white bottle.

"What about the phytoplankton release? It's scheduled to start in one hour." Trevor asked with concern.

"It goes on as planned! And without you!" Thames responded angrily. Walking past each tank he poured a few ounces of bleach into each. It was more than enough to kill anything in the aquariums.

"But, sir, if we test it in San Francisco Bay, there's no turning back. My marine biology doctorate was in invasive species propagation. This species will become invasive. It will out-compete other saltwater phytoplanktons. This phytoplankton could create a carbon trap that could plunge global CO_2 levels over the next several years to unsustainable levels." He gathered his courage and forcefully said, "Sir, this genetically modified life-form could endanger all life on Earth."

Thames gave him an incriminating stare. "It's not your concern anymore. You're being reassigned to take biological samples ... in Patagonia. You leave ... now!"

Twenty years later, Trevor walked alone on a Costa Rican beach. Like the ticking of a slow clock, the floating white foam rushed in with each wave of light green water. Inland the trees were barren of leaves, not from increased global temperature or from rising oceans but from starvation. The carbon trap he helped develop had been all too effective.

32

PETEY AND PAUL

by
Gail Harkins

"Honey, we need to go see Petey." Paul's voice broke as he gazed at the well-worn photo in his hands.

Selma put her arm around his shoulders and took the photo gently from her husband. A baby polar bear stranded on an ice flow stared back. Her eyes widened. "You've named him?"

"Churchill, Manitoba ... The polar bear capital of the world!" Paul opened the hotel room drapes and scanned the streets half expecting a bear to saunter around the corner. "You know, babe, being here's a once-in-a lifetime opportunity. We'll take the bear buggy tour tomorrow, but tonight let's drive out to the trash dump to watch the bears forage."

"Sounds like a plan," Selma responded.

Paul had squeezed this trip into his schedule between the epigenetics symposium he was teaching at the Whitehead Institute and his keynote at the BIO Conference at the end of the week. He wanted to make every moment here count.

That evening Paul and Selma sat in the rented Prius watching bears sift through the debris.

"Oh, look! That one has a cub!" Selma pointed to a sow ripping open a garbage bag.

"They're hungry. More and more are coming in from the wild living off our scraps." Paul's voice was bitter. "The last survey I read indicates the bears are underweight and smaller than they should be. If global warming continues, the population is expected to drop to about 670 in a few more years." He shook his head sadly. "Petey doesn't have a chance ..."

The next day Paul ordered twenty kilos of meat from the butcher. "Make sure it's grass-fed organic beef," he insisted, "and package it in biodegradable paper."

While it was being prepared, he bought a tent, a sleeping bag, and a backpack, and he rented a red pickup truck. When the beef was ready, Paul packed it in a cooler, kissed Selma goodbye, and steered his rented truck out of Churchill.

The Canadian Shield was impossibly flat. The boreal forest had become taiga, devoid of trees, and cut with rivulets and tarns from the last ice age. *It's so beautiful! So barren ... and ... so ... empty.* The sun was well above the horizon when he pulled to the side of the road and pitched his tent that evening. Tomorrow, the adventure would begin.

Bright sunlight coming through the tent woke him.

Reaching for his glasses, he checked his watch. 4:30 a.m. *Does morning always come so early?* Sliding out of his bag, he pulled on a jacket and sneakers, left the tent, and ate the turkey sandwich he had bought yesterday in Churchill. He smiled savoring the task before him.

Others talk about how global warming is hurting polar bears, but I'm actually doing something to help them.

Paul opened the cooler, transferred twenty kilos of beef to his backpack, and set out into the wilderness. The grass was spring green, and the ptarmigan and terns had returned to their mating grounds. Birds chirping and the wind in his ears were the only sounds.

There are so few bears now ... will I find them?

As he walked, he unzipped his jacket. The meat was warming, too. Gradually, its blood soaked through the canvas of his pack. Every meter or so, a dark red droplet fell to the ground. He scanned the horizon. Nothing moved save the short grass rippling in the breeze.

What's that?

He looked over his right shoulder.

A bear? No. Must be my imagination.

When the sun had passed its zenith, he saw something white ahead of him. It was closing on him quickly. Paul's heart thudded wildly.

He's beautiful! I'll leave the meat on that knoll and run back to watch. Why did he stop? The ground's still trembling. Oh, no...

The powerful blow threw him to the ground as claws tore into his pack. He struggled to rip it off but fumbled with the straps. Hot breath grazed the back of his neck.

"Petey! No!"

After Paul left Churchill, Selma read a report in the Globe & Mail. A recent survey of polar bears indicated their population was sixty-six percent higher than previously estimated. Paul had wanted to bring Petey dinner. Petey, however, had eaten his lunch.

MAD ABOUT SCIENCE

by
Sylvia Stein

Dr. Edward Monroe was a very skilled scientist. He had done all his graduate work at John Hopkins in Baltimore, Maryland, and had dedicated so much time to his work that at times, he seemed like a mad man obsessed with his different theories. Soon he would come to realize that being so into his work would be beneficial to the world around him.

It was 3:00 a.m. in the morning when his cell phone began to ring. Dr. Monroe had not been able to sleep due to the massive rain and flooding in the past few weeks. Luckily for him, his only companion was Isaac, his loyal dog, since his wife Abby and their two boys were out of town in New Jersey visiting relatives. Isaac was barking very loudly, so Dr. Monroe opted to let him go outside. Since he had missed the call, he went back to listen to the message on his phone.

"Dr. Edward Monroe, this is the CDC, the Center for Disease Control. Please call us back immediately."

"Oh, this sounds grave," he said as he began to dial the phone. "Hello, this is Dr. Edward Monroe. I received a call from your office."

"Yes, Dr. Monroe, could you please come to our headquarters immediately?" asked the receptionist.

"Ah, sure," he answered.

"Very well. A black sedan will be picking you up shortly."

And just like that she hung up the phone.

After a few minutes a black sedan came to pick him up.

"Hello, Dr. Monroe," said a very slender woman. "I am Stacy Malloy, and I am the head doctor at the CDC. You must be wondering why we called you?"

"Yes," he answered in a nervous tone.

"Well, you see, Doctor Monroe, there seems to be some contaminant causing an outbreak as of late." As she spoke her voice suddenly began to shake.

"Dr. Malloy, are you okay?"

But it was too late. She was not responding.

"Quick!" he called out to her driver. "We must take her to the CDC Lab at once to find out what is wrong with her. Sadly for Dr. Monroe, the driver had also passed out in the front seat.

He could not believe what was happening. It seemed like a bad nightmare. "Oh, I must get down to the CDC and find out what is happening at once!" Dr. Monroe immediately dialed the phone to try and reach his wife and his two boys.

"Honey," he said nervously. "Are you okay?"

"Edward," she cried out, "what is going on?"

"Listen, honey, please stay calm," he added.

"Calm, Edward, how do you expect me to stay calm? I woke up to take Joey to get a glass of water. I noticed the faucet was not working. But the worst part was when my Aunt Rita told me that the local news announced that we could not touch the water due to contaminant that could be fatal. Please, Edward, I am scared, and so are the boys. Come for us. Now!" she cried.

"Honey, I will, but I have to find out how I can help with all of this before more lives get lost. Please trust me."

" Okay," she added hesitantly.

"I promise I will take care of this." He raced against time to try and figure out what to do. Suddenly massive hail began to fall out of the sky. He smiled, "Oh, I have an idea."

Dr. Monroe drove into the CDC Lab and quickly grabbed his notebook of all his formulas and solutions. He went through all the different theories and then began to test them one by one. It only took a few hours before he found the right one when they began to get better. Sadly it was too late for Dr. Malloy and her driver. The serum was quickly updated and sent to different labs around the world. The FDA placed an immediate approval of it due to the massive outbreak in the water.

After an investigation was conducted, it was uncovered that a water line had caused the contamination in the water streams due to the climate changes and the massive flooding. Dr. Edward Monroe's career only got more and more successful, and he was known all over the United States as a hero. After the outbreak, he realized his most important role was of a father and a husband. As he enjoyed time with his family, he was certainly glad he had been a man that was *mad about science.*

34

EXODUS

by
Lynette White

Elrod Lightfoot was an anomaly. His 4' 1" height was the only average thing about him. The average manling was content tending their crops, flocks, and family. They welcomed anyone into their village to trade, but they rarely ventured too far from home themselves. Elrod maintained a home in his native village and would return to it every couple of months. Before long his wandering spirit made him restless, and he would be gone again. In fact Elrod rarely spent more than a few days in one place.

At this particular moment two hundred refugees were completely dependent on Elrod to reach their destination alive. For four years their village was plagued by drought. Crops were dead, and they were starving when he rode into the village six weeks ago today.

It took the village elders an entire week to convince Elrod to guide them to an area untouched by the drought before the entire village died out. Another three weeks passed before everyone was ready for the exodus to the opposite side of the mountain. Elrod could make this voyage alone in a little over a week, but guiding this many manlings with wagons and livestock was an entirely different thing.

They were two weeks into the journey and still had another one to go before they reached their destination. He carefully plotted the route to make the journey as easy as he could. Still they had to outrun a large prairie fire, navigate treacherous trails, and endure an outbreak of influenza that brought everything to a halt for five days.

They lost four manlings to the influenza, they lost three to an enraged grizzly, and they lost seven members of one family. These were typical losses considering the villagers were losing as many as ten manlings per week due to illness and starvation before the exodus started.

The loss of the family of seven today troubled Elrod. He was becoming attached to these manlings, and that bothered him. Normally he kept his emotional ties to a minimum, and he liked it that way. In fact he could count his true friends on one hand.

The manling camp was a clatter of noise, and a few unnecessary words were spoken. Two hundred refugees buried the family of seven lost earlier in the day. The family was navigating a narrow trail when their horse was spooked, and the wagon plunged into a deep ravine. Three hours were wasted retrieving the bodies, but the manlings refused to leave them behind.

Any other night Elrod would be moving around the developing camp giving orders or helping wherever he was needed. Once he had his tent set up, he decided he needed to clear his head.

That night he made his way to the same boulder where he sat and read the note. In one hand was his pipe and in his other was the note someone slipped into his saddlebag on the first day of the journey. It was simple, and he read it several times since he found it. But now the words troubled him.

Thank you
for not leaving us behind to die.
We would never survive this journey
without you.

He was smoking his pipe and deep in thought when an adolescent manling named Crix Ryarson cautiously approached the boulder Elrod was sitting on.

"Mr. Lightfoot, sir." Crix addressed him in a near whisper.

Elrod slowly brought himself out of his reverie and looked down at the young manling. The note disappeared into his pocket. "You need something, Crix?"

Crix shook his head then motioned toward the rock.

Elrod nodded once, so the boy climbed up beside

him. He waited until Crix was settled to speak. "So, what is on your mind, son?"

The boy looked down at the ground for a moment before he answered. "You know, we lost four to the influenza, we lost three to a grizzly, and we lost seven members of one family. It was not your fault they died today."

Elrod lowered his pipe and nodded. "Yes, I know that. Is that why you wandered over here, boy?"

Crix shook his head. "No, sir."

Elrod was not in the mood for company. "Then what is it?"

Crix paused for a moment. "I just wanted to say thank you for helping us. We would not have survived much longer if we stayed where we were, but I knew you would not leave us there to die. I just thought maybe you needed to hear someone say it."

A smile slowly appeared on Elrod's face. He knew now who had slipped that note into his saddle bag. "Thank you, Crix."

35

THE OLD SCHOOL

by
Janet Bond

Jan wiped sweat from her forehead. The sun was hot, and the walk back from the store was long.

"Hey Jessie, let's rest for a while at the old school."

Jessie looked up at his big sister with a frown on his face. "Mom says we're not suppose to go anywhere near the old school."

"You afraid?"

"Well ..."

"It's just an old school. They closed it because it got too hot, and they didn't have the money to get air conditioners."

"Is it haunted?"

"Of course not. Come on. I gotta get out of this sun for a while."

Jan walked through the knee high dry grass towards the school's front door. Jessie paused for a moment at the sidewalk's edge not wanting to go in the school. He waited long enough for Jan to get far away from him.

Suddenly he decided that being alone was worse than going in the school.

The entrance had been a marvel of brickwork—massive square pillars, an arch over the door, windows framed, and steps in three colors. The acidity of the air had taken its toll on the mortar, and the heat had baked out the colors. Jan and Jessie made their way carefully up the steps, stumbling a few times on the stairway's loose bricks.

Jan opened the heavy door. It made a crackling sound. The air inside was cooler but stale. Jessie grabbed two bricks to prop the door open.

They walked down the hallway leaving footprints in the dust of twenty years.

"Look!" said Jan pointing to a sign.

TEACHERS ONLY

"You want to go in?" asked Jan.

"No. I'm not a teacher."

"There aren't any teachers now," said Jan. "I bet you there's a nice chair to sit on."

Jan opened the door and went in. Jessie watched from the doorway.

The room was empty. Jan lost the bet.

A window slammed shut. Jan nearly knocked Jessie over running from the room. They ran towards the exit, but halfway there the door slammed shut with a crash.

They slid to a stop, Jessie running into Jan and sending them both to the floor.

"I knew it!" cried Jessie.

"This way. Quick! We can get out the back."

They started running. The wind started whistling down the hallway. It sounded like the wind said, *Le-e-e-ave*. Jan hit the backdoor at a full run. Jessie was right behind her and jumped down the four steps in a single bound.

They didn't stop running until they were all the way home with the front door closed behind them.

"What have you two been up to?" greeted Mother. "It's way too hot, and you to are way too lazy to be running."

They collapsed on the floor by the door gasping for breath.

"Well ..."

"It was Jan's idea."

Jan shot Jessie a dirty look.

"Well, Jan?" asked Mother.

"It was hot," said Jan.

"And?" asked Mother.

"I wanted to rest for a minute," explained Jan. "We were by the old school."

"It's haunted," added Jessie.

"Didn't I tell you guys not to go there?" questioned Mother.

"Yes, Mother," they replied in unison.

"Now you've gone and made the spirits angry.

You're going to have to go back and apologize. Each of you go get a piece of paper and a pencil."

Jan and Jessie ran from the room and returned with the items. Mother had them write a note to explain why they had bothered the ghosts and how sorry they were.

That evening when it was cooler, the three of them went back to the school. The wind was still howling and Jan was sure it was telling them to *stay away*.

"Take this metal bowl and put your notes in it," instructed Mother.

Jan took the bowl and set it on the ground in front of the main entrance. She put her note in the bowl. Then Jessie added his note to the bowl.

Mother handed Jan a lighter. "Now light it."

Jan hesitated but did as her mother had said. The wind blew out the lighter three times before she was able to get the notes lit. They burned slowly. The smoke swirled in the wind. A gust of wind picked up the ashes and drew them into the air. The ashes swirled and disappeared into thin air.

"Now close the door," directed Mother.

Jan held the door while Jessie removed the two bricks. She let the door close, and it slammed shut. They both jumped.

"Now run along home," ordered Mother.

Jan and Jessie took off running. Mother followed at a much slower pace smiling to herself.

BUT A VIKING'S TALE

by
Scott Amis

13 December 1089, Southeastern France

Horror greeted knight Thierré de Coudre as he rushed into Père Barnard's quarters. The priest sat headless in an armchair, and his desk was splattered with brains, blood, and bone. Thierré pulled a parchment map from the congealing mess. Fresh ink ran and dripped with the blood and gobbets. He drew his cloak close and clattered down dim stone stairs to the stable.

Outside the fortress walls, he spurred his stallion into howling wind and burning sheets of snow and sleet. As he rode into the paupers' graveyard, he saw that the graves of the three highwaymen hanged two weeks before lay open.

Thierré nursed his horse down the trail to Bandits Road, then gave him his head and rode by landmarks through blasts of snow and ice. He spotted the dim lights of his father's manor house, galloped across the half-acre front court, and threw the oaken door open. His brother Galien sprang from his seat before the great room fire but their father Henri only stared into the flames. "Galien, dress and arm for a fight. I'll have your horse saddled and find torches. We need ride to the forest, posthaste."

Galien, at seventeen five years Thierré's junior and his military subordinate, jumped to obey. Shortly, the brothers rode into the maelstrom. They paused at the sheltering west wall of the house. Thierré passed his wine flask. Galien drank. "The Devil bade you drag me out into this. Mother's upstairs dying!"

"God rest her, but we cannot ignore great peril. You remember the curse Berthilde made after the bandits were hanged?"

"I stood beside you, dolt. The hag took horse and none could catch her before she fled into our forest."

"We must kill her. The curse she cast upon us looks to be coming to pass."

"Pig slop. She's a crazy witch healer and her curse but a Viking's tale."

"Had you seen what's left of Père Barnard, you'd be under your bed."

"Père Barnard's dead?"

"Murdered abominably. He told me that the highwaymen's graves were open and drew directions to Berthilde's lair, but they lay ruined in his blood and brains." Galien paled. "I'll enter hell should you order and trust you'll lead us out."

"As I trust you."

They spurred their horses toward the dark forest. Near the treeline, they dismounted. The horses reared, jerked free, and bolted. Thierré drew his longsword. "Let's go in."

Though the old oaks cut the wind, ice-burdened limbs splintered and crashed to the ground. Galien sparked a torch. They moved with caution in the sputtering light. Thierré pointed with his sword. "That's one of the caves. I'll go in." Galien fired another torch and Thierré crept through the low opening. He returned in minutes. "Nothing. I know only of this cave. We'd be fools to venture farther."

Outside the forest, the wind and sleet bit, their horses nowhere in sight. Thierré brought out his flask. Warmed, they started the half-mile trudge to the house and stable. Thierré grinned. "Perhaps Berthilde's curse is naught but a tale."

"Likely. I'm glad you're here. Father needs all of us."

Near frozen, they reached the house. Their horses trod uneasy in the front court. In the dim stable a dark hulking shape brushed Galien. He turned. A rotting corpse swayed before him, stinking of death, war-hammer raised for a lethal blow. Two dark figures jumped Thierré. He stumbled, recovered, and split a decaying head. The monster didn't stop. It swung a rusted sword and Thierré cut it in half at the waist. The second grabbed his left forearm and sunk claws into the chainmail. Blood splattered as Thierré ripped his arm free, drew back his sword, and thrust. The abomination flailed and gurgled, impaled to the wall.

Thierré looked to Galien. He was crouched shield-up, fending off splintering hammer-blows. Thierré picked up the rusted sword and made for the fiend. The witch Berthilde took form before him. She cackled. "Kill me while your brother dies!" Thierré slapped her aside with mail-gloved hand and struck the corpse at the neck. A head rolled, and the body collapsed beside Galien. As Thierré finished the corpse still thrashing on his sword, Berthilde ascended screeching from the floor to vanish into smoke.

Inside the house, the brothers staggered up the staircase. Henri gazed at them from their dying mother's bedside. "Boys, I woke from a horrible dream—living corpses attacked you."

Thierré smiled. "Rest easy, father. We were outside, searching for damage from the storm. You had only a bad dream."

CHAPTER 3

CARNIVALS

37

REFLECTION

by
Arlene Lagos

Five faithful years together, and he plans to shack up with my best friend. I was lucky enough to glance over at a text that backstabbing harlot sent to him. It read:

Meet me at the carnival.

My anger rose inside my chest as he exited the apartment. His lips dripped with lies about having to go to work on a Saturday. I was furious! How could she try and steal my boyfriend from me?

Arriving at the town park, I was full of bad intentions. Pulling my hat down further until it touched the top of my sunglasses, this made it easy for me to go unnoticed while I could get my proof.

I walked around but couldn't find them. Then I thought I caught a glimpse of the back of Jason walking into the house of mirrors. There was a girl in front of him with blonde hair. Her face was hidden, but I knew it was Jenna.

She has been my best friend since we were kids. How could she do this to me? They walked in further, and then I made my way inside. When I entered I could hear giggling so I followed the sound until it led me to a room that I couldn't get out of.

Suddenly it went dark and I heard a voice in the shadows.

"This isn't how you want this to end. You should sit down and talk with Jason. Give him a chance to explain," the voice said.

"Who's there?" I asked.

"Give him a chance to explain? What other explanation could there be for him being on a date with her best friend? He's obviously cheating. You should never trust anyone," a second voice said.

"I'm scared in here. Can someone turn on the light?" I whimpered.

"You don't have all the facts. You should ask him point blank why he is here with her," a third voice said.

"Oh, like he's really going to tell her the truth!" the second voice said.

"I'm sure there's a perfectly good explanation. You don't have to be so negative all the time," the first voice said.

"Stop talking!" I yelled. "Who are you people? What's going on?" I asked.

A light flickered in the distance casting a shadow upon three mirrors all reflecting images. They were images of me. There was one of me crying, one of me angry, and one of me happy.

"I don't understand. How can this be happening?" I asked.

"We are you, all three of us, all the time. We help you make your decisions based on your intellect, your emotions, and your rationality," they said in unison.

"But I am still confused. I don't know what to do?" I cried.

"Do what you always do."

"Don't do anything."

"Try something new."

A breeze floated by me. Then a butterfly wisped through a crack in the doorway. It compelled me to follow. I stayed on its trail where it eventually led me to the exit. Catching my breath I stood shaking and trying to digest what just happened.

Across the park I saw Jason again. He was standing on a sound stage putting up a banner. Jenna was there too. As I watched them laughing and joking with each other, I began to cry and clench my fists in rage. The thoughts running through my head were scrambled, and I honestly wasn't sure what I was going to do when I reached them.

Breathing heavier now, I became lightheaded from the emotional state I was in and could barely contain the tears ready to burst from my eyes. I had to stop for a moment and close them before I passed out.

After a few minutes I got my bearings. I lifted my head and moved toward the sound stage until I saw something that stopped me dead in my tracks. A brightly colored banner hung perfectly across the top of the stage with the words splashed across it:

Michelle, will you marry me?

My jaw dropped as I stood there in total awe. *He's going to propose to me? He's going to propose to me!*

A swarm of different emotions spilled around inside as my heart sunk deep in my chest. Sitting down on the ground, I hung my head in shame. I had let trust fly out the window without giving it any thought. Now because of my rage, all I felt was embarrassment and shame. Wiping the last tear from my eye, something landed on my knee. It was that same butterfly. It sat there staring at me, and I stared back. This winged creature was beautiful, and it speckled with several colors. I sat speckled with many emotions. It was a symbol of change for an ability to grow emotionally, to create more positive reflections of myself, and to learn to think before I act.

38

CHASING REFLECTIONS

by
Douglas G. Clarke

Go left or right? Chris saw her image looking back at her from the mirror. She looked left toward the narrow corridor as it disappeared into a fog. Both walls vanished into an infinite reflection of each other. To the right the hall was the same. A drop of sweat fell from her brow.

Chris jumped back when a hundred images of Julie flashed on the walls around her and then just as suddenly disappeared. "Julie!" She clenched under her breath.

Left. If I always go left I can't get lost. She turned left and started walking. The fog cleared as she walked further. Then her image walked towards her. It reflected in a mirror twenty feet away.

Crash. Pain shot through her head and arm as she suddenly stopped. "Ouch!"

"Watch out for the glass, stupid. It's not just mirrors." Julie's voice echoed through the room.

Chris took a step back and rubbed her nose. She raised her other hand slowly until her fingertips touched her reflection. She took a step back and ran her fingers along the glass wall.

"I hate you!" Chris yelled. Her left hand trembled as it trailed along the glass. Her right hand tightened into a fist. "Just give me back my ticket." Chris dropped her head. Her body shuddered.

A moment later she took in a deep breath, brought her fist down against her leg, and then lifted her head. She spun, teeth gritted, and moved her right hand to the wall. Extending her left hand in front of her, she walked quickly down the hallway. When her hand dropped away from the wall, she turned. She moved her hand to the left wall and headed down the side passage without slowing. *Another turn. A dead end. Turn. Turn. Dead end. Turn. Dead end.*

"I'm almost through. How about you, loser?"

Chris felt a tightness in her chest as Julie's words echoed around her. Her right hand was a fist again, and she pounded the wall in front of her with it. She stumbled as the floor moved. and she realized that she was turning around. As quickly as it had started, the movement stopped.

"Great," she mumbled. Following the left wall won't work, because the walls were moving. *What now?*

She started walking again with her hand extended but slower than before. *Left. Left. Dead end. Left.* She stopped panting. Chris unfastened the top two buttons of her blouse and fluttered it causing a slight but welcome breeze.

"I hope you get out soon, girlfriend." Julie's hateful laugh seemed to come from everywhere. "I want you to be able to watch me use your ticket. I can't wait to feel his lips on mine. They'll be sweet but even sweeter if you're there."

Chris was almost running. The turns and dead ends blurred into one. She abruptly stopped when Julie's image appeared all around her. *I've got you now.* Chris began running and bouncing off the walls. Julie's image appeared and disappeared. Then her image appeared framed by daylight.

"You lose." Julie vanished into the light.

Chris smashed into another dead end and fell to her knees. Tears ran down her cheeks. She stood up slowly and started to walk back down the hallway. Her arms were outstretched and her eyes cast down. She stepped over a lollipop.

A moment later the importance of it screamed in her head. She spun around and focused on the thin line of ants that ran from it. Chris followed the line, and in a moment she was looking across the fairway toward the kissing booth. She watched in horror as Julie handed her ticket to Robert. Chris was running now, trying to scream, but nothing came out. Robert placed his hand behind Julie's head and pulled her towards him.

Watching in slow motion, the kiss seemed to last forever. Chris reached the booth, stopped, and stared. Julie's kiss was over. She turned around and faced Chris. A smile was on her face. Neither girl spoke.

Julie's smile grew as the blood drain from Chris's face. It appeared Julie was about to say something when another voice stopped her.

"Oh! There you are, Chris. We heard you lost the ticket you bought, so the guys decided to chip in and buy you a new one. Well, we actually we bought ten. Robert stepped pass Julie and put his hand behind Chris's head. His gentle, but firm embrace pulled her to his lips. As they touched, Julie's face went white, but Chris didn't even notice.

39

R U T H – L E S S

by
Laura Stafford

"I didn't mean to lose it!" Lisa sobbed on Mary Jo's shoulder, but I could swear she was winking at me.

I was standing at the entrance to the labyrinth. A black iron gate with weaving ivy was the only way in and the only way out. Calls were echoing over and above me like smoke fading into the air.

"Ruth! Ruth! Answer us! Ruth!"

Counselors, kids, directors, and police were calling, shouting, begging, and questioning.

I was watching Lisa, also known as Mosquito. She was holding Mary Jo's hand. Her voice trembled. Her brown puppy eyes squeezed tears, but Lisa didn't like Ruth to begin with. Was there a gleam in her eye? Was there a twinge of a smile at the corner of her mouth?

* * *

All summer Lisa had clung to me competing with Ruth and making fun of her. We were at this *youth camp for troubled teens* for all the same reasons. Ruth and I were caught smoking on school grounds during lunchtime.

We didn't know Lisa that well. They brought kids here from all across the Tri-County area to learn how to *act responsibly*. Lisa is just some girl who attached herself to us. Ruth calls her Mosquito because she buzzes around, gossips, lies, and whispers in my ear like a mosquito. Every time we swat at her, she circles and returns.

"Ruth called you a b— " Lisa buzzed during campfire songs. "She said it's your fault she got in trouble."

"Ruth told me you're a lesbian," Lisa hummed at breakfast one morning. "Said you tried to kiss her once."

"Ruth says you're a slut," she whispered at the field hockey game. "She says you slept with the whole football team."

But I knew what kind of girl Lisa was. There was a mosquito every summer at every camp my parents sent me to. And I knew what kind of good friend Ruth was. I knew Ruth would never say those things. I didn't even ask.

When we got off the bus at the Crystal Cove Garden

Maze, Lisa was already holding my hand *sucking my blood.*

"Can I walk with you guys? Mary Jo says I have to have a partner," Lisa said to Ruth and me.

"Getting through the maze will be like a mission, a team-building exercise, and sort of like a scavenger hunt," Mary Jo instructed in her squeaky I'm-a-counselor-but-I'm-pretending-to-be-your-friend voice. "Find your way to the center gazebo, and pick up the totem that matches your cabin." Our cabin totem was the bear. She continued. "And return to the picnic table by the bus before four o'clock. The first team out of the maze wins a prize!"

The girls mumbled. They shuffled their feet and rolled their eyes.

My team was in the lead.

Ruth didn't mess around when it came to competition. Lisa was holding us up. She wandered aimlessly, flitting to flowers, benches and ceramic gnomes. She wasn't watching for landmarks or helping us decipher the maze. But we were still the first to the gazebo. All of the totems were there waiting patiently on the bench.

Lisa snatched the bear. "I'll carry it!" She twisted, dragged, and turned aimlessly. Then she sat and wasted time.

Ruth was on a mission to drive and push us. She wanted to move us and lead us out.

"Mary Jo!" Ruth called as she crashed through the gate holding her hand out to Lisa.

"What?" Mary Jo asked from the picnic table.

"What?" Lisa asked.

"Give me the bear," Ruth said behind her.

"We did it!" Lisa said in front of her and shrugged. "I already gave it to you."

"No. You didn't. Where's the stupid bear?"

"I gave it to you," Lisa argued, "in there." She jerked her thumb back towards the entrance to the labyrinth.

"No. You. Didn't. Where's the bear?" I could tell Ruth wasn't just exasperated. She was mad.

Lisa shrugged again. "Then I must have set it down when we stopped."

I could tell Ruth was ready to crush the incessant Mosquito. She darted back in with a growl much like a bear.

"Ruth!" I called, but she was already out of sight.

We waited. Four o'clock came and went. With totems, prizes, and the mission forgotten, we began to search. We called for Ruth and looked in ridiculous places. We looked under bushes, up in trees, behind fences, and we kicked at flowers and even piles of dead leaves. It was as if there were some secret door or passageway that she fell through, like Alice falling down the rabbit hole. But she didn't come out of the labyrinth. There was one way in and one way out. Ruth was gone. Police were called. Parents were informed. Rumors spread. Searches ensued. Police reports followed. Girls were sent home. And I was sent home…Ruth-less.

NIGHTSHADE PARK

by
Kristen Strassel

I slapped away mosquitoes while I waited in the rollercoaster line. There's nothing sexy about being covered in bites.

I adjusted my tank top so it showed just the right amount of cleavage. "You know, Lissy, you're going to fall right out of that on the loop-de-loop." My sister Katie admonished me.

"So what. That will get Mark's attention."

"I'm sure no one has tried that before." Katie snarked. Mark operated the rollercoaster at Nightshade Park. He was probably the most handsome boy I'd ever seen. I'd never seen him around town before this summer. I think he spent the rest of the year at college. Rumors swarmed the park about Mark. He had the attention of every girl in town. My goal was to get them talking about how I was the one who got him.

We reached the front of the line. I insisted on waiting for the front seats. That way I could stare at Mark longer. Katie rolled her eyes. The colored lights put red highlights in his shaggy dark hair and highlighted the muscles in his arms. It was almost more thrilling than the roller coaster.

He operated the machine just inches from where we waited. I smiled at him but didn't say anything. Katie judged my every move.

"Hey." At first I wasn't sure he was talking to me. "Going for front row this time?"

"Sure. The more exciting the better." Katie rolled her eyes as I pushed out my chest.

"The park closes at midnight. Meet me here then."

"Okay." I didn't need a ten-story drop to take my breath away. Mark just did it.

At the end of the night, I told Katie I'd text her when I wanted her to pick me up. "Oh, no way. I'm not leaving you alone with some strange carnie. I don't care how hot he is. We don't know anything about him."

"He didn't invite you, and I'm not looking for an audience. I will text you." I left her speechless when I walked away.

Mark waited alone in the shadows at the entryway to the *Blastcaster Coaster*. The park looked so peaceful empty with the lights still twinkling. He could probably hear my heart pounding as I approached.

"You came alone?" He seemed surprised.

"Yeah, my sister didn't want to come. Is that cool?"

"Of course, I'm just surprised. Girls usually travel in packs. It's nice to get you to myself." I tried not to swoon. He reached for my hand. I took it, surprised by its coolness on this humid night. "Follow me. I have something to show you."

I bet he did. This wasn't my first rodeo or amusement park. Truth be told, I couldn't wait to see whatever it was.

He led me through a door in the fence I'd never noticed in my many trips here every summer since I could walk. We navigated through a narrow passageway formed by more fences. Unusual music grew louder as we made our way down the trail. Once we reached the end, a small village revealed itself. These weren't the squatter houses or trailers you'd expect transient workers to live in. These were elegant villas that almost looked like gingerbread houses. Around the perimeter the tops of the rides still glowed. They were more magical than anything I'd ever seen in the public area of the park.

"Wow. Is this where you're staying this summer?"

"Yes," he said. "Beautiful, isn't it? I'll be here until the end of time."

I wished I could stay right here in this magical oasis with him. "It's the most beautiful place I've ever seen."

"You can stay here, if you like it."

"Are you asking me for a second date, Mark?" I pushed my body against his.

"Something like that." He looked down at me. I'd

never noticed how intense his eyes were before. "Have you ever wondered why the park is only open at night?"

"Because it's called Nightshade Park? It's a gimmick." Everyone knew that.

Mark shook his head and smiled. "Sort of. The real reason is, we can only come out at night."

"What are you trying to say? Are you a—"

I never got to finish before he sunk his teeth into my neck and sucked the life out of me.

41

HALLOWEEN RITUAL

by
Jot Russell

With the help of a black cape, plastic teeth, and my mother's make-up, I set out with the gang for our annual Halloween ritual. The air was cold and the sky seemed to drain all illumination from the foggy surrounding. I had to rely on the voices of the shadowy figures to tell who was able to sneak out. It wasn't a surprise that the loudest was John, who barged over toward me to show-off his fake exoskeleton and matching antennae.

Aside from this bug, I was happy to see Phil displaying himself as an awesome Mad Hatter. Steve was a gladiator, and Jim dressed as a winged bat. Joe was the same green-faced hoodlum he was each year.

As we passed through the large metal gates guarding the circular labyrinth of graves and mausoleums, our voices quickly faded, and the pace of our steps slowed to a crawl. With the gang drawing closer together, I noticed the tension building. Once we passed the first large structure, I screamed, "Ahhh!"

I laughed at John who jumped the furthest.

"Hey, who took my hat?" Phil complained.

I looked around to see everyone shooting glances at each other. With our hands out we looked back at Phil. He turned and glared at me. "This is your doing. I knew we should have left you behind!" Pushing me aside, he walked off alone into the dark mist in search of his hat.

"Guys, this is serious. Who threw his hat?" I asked.

After a few seconds of silence and blank stares, a deafening scream erupted in the faint distance. It was not the false cry that I had projected, but a sound that immediately sank into the fear receptacles of my soul.

We scattered away like rats. I ran and dodged the maze of headstones eventually tripping over a loosely dug hole. I landed face first in a rotten bouquet of flowers that lay in front of a large stone that read:

William Lawrence Russell
3-13-1831 to 10-31-1900
Maryland Asylum for the Insane

As I sat there trembling at the sight of my own family name on the headstone, another scream erupted. I pulled my feet from the mangled hole that led down towards the grave of what I could only assume to be my great-great-grandfather. I tried to clear my memory of the sight as I ran, but the image remained painted before me in the fog.

Finally, I found my way to the tall metal gate, but it was locked. I yanked on the bars to no avail. Echoes of the rattle caused me to halt and face back into the mist.

There was the faintest sound of a footstep. Looking into the fog, I saw a figure. It was more like a darkening gray within a cloud. I didn't wait to verify its form. Making a mad dash along the perimeter, I sought out a break in the fence or some type of hidden passageway.

Another deadly scream caused me to pause and subdue my fears. My heavy breaths broke the silence that I strained to create. The next unearthly echo cured me of even my need to breathe. I stood there and struggled against the burning in my lungs. The fifth scream was also different in texture, but this one I knew to be John.

I stood there waiting, not knowing where to run. Like a bat in the dark, silent and erratic, a small object was cast toward me. By instinct I caught the blood stained antennae cap that John had worn. Startled it fell from my hands as I turned to run.

The hollow sockets within the decayed face cast down from the form that lay in my path. Like magnets against my will, my eyes locked into his empty orifices as his leather-shrouded hands clenched around my throat. He leaned closer showing his lipless mouth arranged with broken and jagged teeth. I watched the parting of his jaw drawing ever close to my face. As his jaw moved back together, a haunting breeze emanated from his mouth.

"Russell," he rasped.

I fell to the ground with the release of his grasp and saw him stagger back in the direction of his grave. Sitting there cold and helpless in the madness of the night, I wondered if William's fate would become my own.

42

THE IMPENDING DEATH

OF

HARLEQUIN

by
Richard Bunning

The Carnival Theatre's season ends, and for me the prospect of Lent seems even grimmer than usual. I already miss sweet Columbine. What is worse than her lack of love for me is her new interest in that jester—that butterfly winged Harlequin. More like a stinking moth . . . if only. I have to concede to his looks, he certainly turns the girls' heads. Even Dorothy the fire-eater, who usually only has eyes for her own kind, seems to have taken a shine to that Harlequin. Whatever his attraction, his mannerisms, his looks, or perhaps just being in tune with their banter, it works.

I let myself believe that Columbine and I . . . All that

time spent helping plan her routine, to now feel so rejected.

Oh Columbine,

> *Like a drum my heart was beating,*
> *and your kiss was sweet as wine.*
> *But the joys of love are fleeting*
> *for Pierrot and Columbine.*

It isn't only the end of this Carnival, but the last one for me. I don't think I could stand another season without Columbine. Or even worse, one where she's with Harlequin.

> *Now the harbour light is calling,*
> *this may be our last goodbye.*
> *Though the Carnival is over*
> *I will love you till I die.*

Stolen love, that's what it is. I feel every bit as bad now as I did when the trailer was trashed, my stuff pinched. No, actually I feel much worse. I just can't believe I trusted that Harlequin. I mean, he seemed so camp that never for a minute did I see him as a rival. I never thought that he would . . . could.

I could kill him . . . I'll make him pay.

The *how* is the question.

Accidents happen during performances, even to comic comperes like Harlequin. Theatre, especially when some circus is involved, has a long history of *accidents*. I like the idea of his dramatic final exit in front of an audience. I wonder if, with a little planning, his final act can take place when I have already departed. If I am already out at sea, then even if they tie me to the crime I will be out of easy reach.

What do I know about that pathetic butterfly? . . . I know, I know exactly what needs doing. Time is short. Tonight I must act. First I'll take a trip out of town, to Beelzebub's Honey Farm. Then after a quick stop at the theatre I'll still have time to get to the docks.

What do I need: a cold-box to carry my unwitting assassins, some newspaper to keep the ice-blocks off the creatures? When cool they are calm, huddled together. Then I need a face net, a stocking might do. Well that is easy. There is a pair of laddered tights in the trash-bin in the trailer. Columbine left them, that night ... I can use the fine nylon over my pantomime mask. With gloves as well that will prevent most stings.

It is a chilly night. The bees will be calm. Yes, I can do it. There is time. Then I will leave the cold-box, uncovered except with cling-film. Just enough slits for air but enclosed enough that the bees get warm. By the matinee they should be very agitated, very angry. All the noise on stage, will ensure that no one hears them buzzing. I can imagine the agitated bees under the trap door that only Harlequin ever uses. When he drops, suddenly down, disappears from the stage. Brilliant! Angry bees will cause mayhem.

CARNIVALS

You stupid fool! You never should have told me how you so nearly died of anaphylactic shock. This time there will be no helping you. And me, I will already be at sea, on a fortnights cruise. I can jump ship, in half a dozen ports. What is there for me here, without the love of Columbine?

> *High above the dawn is waiting*
> *and my tears are falling rain.*
> *For the Carnival is over,*
> *we may never meet again.*

Yes, I must start now. Time is marching on. He will only wake beside my Columbine one more time . . .

Here they are, two cruise tickets. I will leave Columbine's, abandoned with my hopes.

Death through misadventure with bees will be a suitably end to this tragic play.

43

BAKE & THE PREDATOR

by
Alli Vaughan

Bake chewed his lower lip as he stared at the distorted figures surrounding him. They shivered and melded into a sea of silver. Though they were mindless and grotesque products of light and illusions, he didn't falter before them.

"What are you doing?" Shelia barked and grabbed his arm sharply. His eyes dropped from the array of mirrors.

"Sorry," he mumbled to his wife.

"This is your fault, so stop screwing around! We need to find the bag and get out of here." With that she stormed off toward the entrance to the fun house.

"You mean before the cops find us," he whispered under his breath.

"This way." She hissed and pulled him into the dark.

An animated gypsy welcomed the couple to the

House of Madness. Unease gripped him as he passed monkeys with rolling heads and women balancing on thin ropes. Shelia stormed through the house and rudely pushed people out of her way in her quest to find the lost item.

"Watch it!" She screamed at a plump man standing with his child who didn't move in time.

The fat man stared wide-eyed. His eyes were still adjusting to the dark.

Sheepishly he scooted to the side. "Sssssorry," the man stuttered.

Bake frowned.

"There it is!" Shelia said as she placed her hand to her thin hip. "Get in there and get it!"

Bake waded compliantly into the ball pit and crawled in search of the lost bag. Grasping a thin handle, he pulled it up. Shelia snatched it out of his hand. "Great, now let's sneak out the side."

"Side?" He asked. When they had come through earlier today, he thought there had only been the entrance and the exit.

"Where the staff exits," she said slowly. Sheila couldn't believe how dumb he was.

As if it were a magical portal, Shelia found an exit where a wall had been. It opened into a long passage. Bake walked slowly ahead. Guilt started to flood him. He pinched his eyes as the memory of today's robbery and all the blood. Shelia went overboard spilling blood on the bank's stone floor. He couldn't keep this up.

Stealing was one thing, but Bake wouldn't kill anyone.

As he moved through the tunnel lost in thought, a cold metallic object pressed on his neck.

"That's far enough," Shelia's voice cut through the air.

"What's going on?" He asked, already knowing the answer to his question. He should have known. Slowly he shuffled around to face her. Even in the darkness, her green eyes glowed like firelight.

"You didn't think this would last, did you, Bakey?" Her voice laughed and mocked him as she ran her fingernails over his chest.

"I guess part of me did," he said. "But I would have given you all of the money, Shelia."

"It's not just that. A praying mantis always seals her lover's fate," Shelia said before she fired the trigger at his chest.

Bake stumbled out of the passage. Blood dripped down his pants. The ground seemed to run at him as he walked sideways back to the line of mirrors. Distorted smiles offered him the relief he had been waiting for. He greeted the figures as friends. They stepped out of their silvery background to surround him with supportive hands.

THE KING'S SECRET

by
Harry Alexiou

Joel was hesitant at first, but the others had convinced him to go. He was their best fighter and the strongest they had. Once he'd confirmed that Miranda would be going too, he was more agreeable almost enthusiastic.

Miranda stood at the entrance clearly unhappy with the lumbering assistant chosen for such an important journey. Nobody had ever been into the labyrinth and for good reason. The legendary resident of the lair had never been seen, but many had heard it as it noisily devoured its meals night after night in the depths of the steaming habitat. The foul stench occasionally wafted across to the village depending on the direction of the winds. Southerly was bad, and northerly was good.

A giant Coleoptera had taken something that hadn't been offered by the villagers. An agreement had been broken, and now their survival depended on the return of the Golden Orb.

Ursula's blood boiled as she stood amongst the crowd and watched powerless. Her eyes threw daggers at Miranda. "May the gods be with you!" Ursula called out directing her wish to Joel. He smiled, but his expression belied his inner fear as he turned to enter the labyrinth behind Miranda.

The Queen of all Carinthia looked at the intricately carved door that had been bolted by the King as it was every night. It was just his way. He always insisted that the only way to get a good night's sleep was alone. She settled down for the night and prayed that the villagers would be successful. The King needed to regain support and settle the negative mood stirring amongst them.

Miranda and Joel had cautiously made their way deep into the maze of tunnels, but there was still no sign of the Orb or the thief. Joel had his hand firmly grasped around the hilt of his sword. His weapon had been forged using the toughest Carinthia steel. Its tip had been custom hardened to penetrate the tough exoskeleton of the Coleoptera.

"Miranda," started Joel, "you know that I—"

"Ssshhh!" she exclaimed and raised a hand. Her hearing was exceptional, but Joel heard nothing. She could hear something like the breaking of bones or sticks. She pointed forward and to his sword.

Joel was a well-trained swordsman, but his opponents had always been of flesh and blood. He took the lead, visibly trembling, and tried to steady his grip on his weapon.

They inched forward peering down partly lit tunnels attempting to pinpoint the source of the noises. They stopped dead. They listened. Their eyes were wide with fear. Joel's knuckles whitened, and his firm grip threatened to cut the flow of blood to his fingers. He released his grip slightly but clumsily let the sword clatter to the ground. The sound echoed around them. They froze. Both stopped breathing. Their eyes darted from side to side.

The blood-curdling shriek preceded by the appearance of the oversized beetle. It gave no warning as its shiny black jaws clamped around Miranda's waist and dragged her backwards into the dark depths.

Joel would never forget her screams and the look of horror on her face as she disappeared still holding the torch.

He stumbled back screaming her name and fell into one of the darkened tunnels tumbling endlessly downwards. Joel came to an abrupt halt and lay motionless. The last two minutes of his life had been horrific, and he fought to assimilate all the information.

Miranda was dead. Was he dead? In the pitch black of the tunnel, he felt a slight wisp of air. He sat up, raised his hand, and felt his bloodied head.

Joel groaned and blindly groped around for his

sword. As his eyes adjusted, he noticed a sliver of light. He momentarily forgot about his sword and Miranda. He moved toward the light that came from a solid wooden panel. An intricately carved door confronted Joel. Feeling the edges, he made out two bolts and quietly slid them open. Joel opened the door and stared in disbelief.

45

THE BEACH BUNKER

by
Oliver Dolan

Charlie got off the bus at First Street, crossed Coastal Highway, and was on the Boardwalk within minutes. He was alone walking quickly. He lit a smoke and stepped in line for Festival Pier Theme Park where the boardwalk ended. Festival Pier had been there since the sixties, and Charlie had been there many times as a boy.

Walking back through the park years later was weird for Charlie. The rides now looked old and rusty, the operators were old, and the crew seemed creepy. High school kids worked the restaurants and cleaned the park.

Charlie soon realized how hungry he'd become on his journey down and walked over to the concession stand with a fresh Philly cheesesteak and creamy chocolate milkshake on his mind.

A middle-aged man wearing dark sunglasses, a bright purple suit, and a zebra print top hat approached Charlie's picnic table. He introduced himself and said, "Hello there, sir. My name is Sylvester Stuard or Sly Stu. I am a professional magician. I propose that you allow me to let you in on an incredible magic trick that is, in fact, reality. It will cost $100. I'd ask you to accept, but you've actually already accepted my offer. You are a wise one."

A startled Charlie felt his blood run cold as he realized his wallet was no longer in his back pocket.

Sly Stu continued. "You came here alone, son, didn't you? No one ever comes here alone. If they do, I talk to them and offer this arrangement. It is the same one you have already accepted my friend."

Charlie tried to intervene, but Stu completely ignored him and continued in a forceful whisper. "Eat your food. Then report immediately to the oldest ride in the park. You'll instinctively know what to do."

Stu, wearing a toothy smile, stood up, tipped his cap, and left Charlie alone with his thoughts.

Charlie devoured his food and sprinted for the Ferris Wheel by the ocean. As he approached the ride he saw a blue door slightly cracked open. Without thinking he sped inside.

Charlie looked around and focused his attention on the steel door in the back right corner that was covered with huge African Killer Bees. Charlie approached the door with caution. To the left he saw a white sign which read:

COURAGE IS AN ANGEL
AND
PATIENCE IS A VIRTUE

With this Charlie walked toward the door. It was locked. Staring the bees in the face, he unlocked it. Easing the door open, the bees began to land on his fingertips and neck. He slipped through a two-foot crack he'd created, and the bees slowly flew away.

He stumbled and nearly fell as he realized that a pitch-black staircase was beyond the sturdy steel door. Luckily Charlie was a smoker. He instantly pulled out his lighter and lit a torch that was hanging on the dark wall to his right.

Charlie continued down the stairs and through a long dark tunnel. Just as he considered turning around, he saw the sun's rays beaming through some dune grass at the end. The flat rocks that had been beneath his shoes turned into sand. He ditched the torch and took off his shoes. He crawled through the dune grass into the bright beautiful sunlight.

Charlie arose from the ground. All fright inside of him was blown away with the crisp bay breeze. He saw an empty beach, a calm ocean, a hammock, a small hut, and a palm tree. On the tree there was a long sign made out of ocean-tattered wood. It read:

Welcome to the Beach Bunker. This is not what you came to find. This found you. There is a cellar with a lifetime's supply of everything you might want or need. But you should know that on this Beach Bunker time does not pass. So clear your mind and become at peace within. Let all your hostilities fly away. Anything you'd like to say while here, write it down. Be at ease. You are on a vacation from reality, young seedling.

Overtaken with emotion, Charlie collapsed to his knees, and then to his stomach. The sun was setting, and the sky filled with mind-blowing hues of pinks, oranges, and blues.

He closed his eyes and fell asleep within thirty seconds without anything on his mind. He just felt happy. He felt at peace. He'd never been so alone, and he'd never been so alive.

46

CANDY CARNIVAL

by
H. M. Schuldt

An extremely rare carnival worker recently vanished from a privately owned traveling carnival, Fancy Pants. The missing person bore the name of Candace Lynn Denham, also known as Candy. She performed in the knife-throwing act with her brother, Brooks, who had been successfully performing in one of the main attractions for almost a whole year. Candy had come to dread her part after just two weeks in the summer.

"Brooks, I don't want you throwing knives at me anymore. I want to be in the Procession," Candy said before she went missing.

"I can't keep an eye on you if you're with the drummers. Can't you be happy with something for once? The knife throwing act is one of the main shows here," Brooks said. "Besides, the owner already has a Queen in the Procession."

Coming from a family with old money, Candy and Brooks went against the tradition of working for the family newspaper. Mother complained to the town ladies about her children who had grown from an adventurous free spirit to hitting an all time low by joining the travelling carnival full of cons and cheats.

This happened last summer when Brooks graduated from college. Mother was shocked to find out about his accurate ability to throw knives. She tried her best to show the utmost disgust for filthy concessions and low life carnival workers, but Brooks took the job knowing he wouldn't get his hands dirty. Candy heard her brother's small attempt of trying to assure Mother as best as he could that he would be dressed fine in a pinstripe suit and that his knives have a safe landing. It didn't work. Brooks had a healthy glow, but he wasn't much of a talker or a convincer. Mother still didn't approve. She continued to be sickened, but she bought Brooks a motorhome anyway.

Candy was an original, classy as all get out. She was a real talker, and she held an expensive taste for clothing and wigs. One year out of high school, her main problem was that college life had not been entertaining enough. She held no interest for textbooks or listening to know-it-all professors lecture about psychology and political science. The carnival sounded alive, and it would be her goal to stay at the *ten-in-one* if Brooks was there.

Not everyone is chosen at Fancy Pants as a carney. The owner searched real hard to find talent for the freak show—an extremely fat singing lady and a one-legged belly dancer. Other carneys were easier to find— buccaneer acrobats and stilt walkers who wore the carnival's *fancy pants*. The owner, Fireball Deborah, went to great lengths to find the best talkers. These talkers include inside talkers to lure patrons into buying more tickets and outside talkers to sell tickets for the carnival as a ballyhoo.

Brooks's knife throwing talent landed him a job that came all too easy. The owner was on the hunt for more roughies, and Brooks had an ageless personality that brought in new talent. Candy, on the other hand, was brought in by her stunning looks and carney attitude, valuable enough to play a mark.

The day before Fancy Pants opened in Lafayette, Brooks endured a practice round with Farley the Fur Man. Farley stood against the bull's eye target with his arms to the side. Fur hung down at least twelve inches from his arms. He stood there pinned to the target because Fireball Deborah demanded that Farley had to fill in for Candy. Other carneys spread the word to look around for a better substitute. Farley protested, "This costume is too hot! He's cutting off my fur!"

At last, Sarina the two-legged belly dancer arrived to take Farley's place.

Fireball Deborah quickly came to terms with how Brooks wanted his sister in the carnival. No one knew where Candy was hiding except for the spoof of all spoofs, Fireball Deborah. Inside Fireball's trailer far away from the center joint and down a secret passageway, Candy and Fireball came up with a move that everyone would be happy with, even Candy's Mother.

The next day Fancy Pants opened in Lafayette where drummers marched to a steady beat. Giant insect balloons hovered over the crowd as lemonade and cotton candy vendors walked up and down the street. Newspaper reporters and photographers stood ready to find an opportune moment. Just behind the stilt walkers came a royal throne float with the *King and Queen of Fancy Pants*. Cameras flashed as the crowd waved back.

The next day Mother opened the family newspaper and was impressed by the headline. "Henry! Come look what the kids have been up to. You might be the king of our newspaper, but Brooks and Candy are the *King and Queen of Fancy Pants.*"

47

BUBBLE BOY

by
Randy Dutton

Billy's transparent bubble bounced thirty meters as his entourage of laughing children, each in their own bubble, rolled and bumped across the small lunar crater.

He didn't just want to lead. He wanted to entertain. As a finale, he scrambled up the inflatable moon ball's interior and forced the orb into a rapid spin. As the specially designed touring ball hit the dusty surface, the ball's ribs gripped the surface. It forced a direction change that ricocheted him off one boulder then another, just like an antique pinball machine.

The final bounce pocketed him inside the air lock just as he had practiced a thousand times. Through speakers he heard a final round of applause from the paying guests as orbs settled into *egg carton* depressions.

With doors opening and closing, lights flashing, and the cacophony of whooshing air and announcements, the ride ended. Everyone exited, everyone except Billy. Still smiling he rolled his bubble to a specially designed container connected to his apartment.

Within moments his bubble was sanitized, and he stepped into his sterile abode alone except for Cricket. The insect chirped a greeting from his armchair. She was one of many generations he had raised on Earth and the Moon.

"Hi, Billy!" Angela announced via video link. She was his friend and co-worker.

"Hello, Angela!" He responded excitedly.

"Seems you're still everyone's favorite adventure!"

"I enjoy taking people on a moon bounce. I feel closer to the visitors bubble-to-bubble than watching them on a monitor."

She hesitated. "Like when we talk face-to-face?"

With hopeful eyes and pursed lips, he nodded. "May I?"

She looked side-to-side and then coquettishly nodded. "I've got something for you."

Billy grinned. "Be right there!"

He ran to the vent and pulled off the cover. He crawled into the ventilation supply network and arrived at a louver cover.

Outside the vent a beautiful redhead sat in a swivel chair pretending to read an eTablet while taking in the purified air. At her feet was a box of sanitizer wipes.

"You look beautiful as always, Angela," Billy said dreamily.

She peered at the barely lit face and smiled. She picked up a wipe and thoroughly sanitized her hand. She slipped her fingers through two louvers.

He gently held her fingers then pressed his lips to them. His eyes misted. "I've missed your touch."

"Billy, you're important to me, but this is dangerous."

"I've lived twenty-two years with Severe Combined Immunodeficiency. SCID. And for two years I've held your hand and haven't caught any germs. What makes you think that'll change?"

She sniffed. "Because I want more. I need more."

"So do I, but *more* would kill me. Can't we just continue talking and touching like this?"

"I've met a guy from Systems Analysis," she stammered.

"That doesn't mean we can't visit." She breathed deeply.

"He's rotating back to Earth next month. He wants to get married."

"I didn't expect—"

She gently pulled her fingers out. "But that's not the surprise."

"What then?" he asked.

"We have a new hire coming. I think you'll like her. They want you to teach her." Angela said.

"She's not you."

"I know, but she also has SCID with the same muscular degeneration you suffered."

"So bubble boy meets bubble girl?"

"You can be together. Don't you want someone you can be with physically?"

"I've always wanted you."

"If there was anyway, you know I'd make it happen."

"Angela, you've been my best friend. I don't want to lose you."

"We'll stay in contact. I'm sorry."

After a moment's silence, he pushed a locket through the louver.

"Angela, I fished it from your desk. Sorry, I just wanted something of yours."

"Billy!" With a wipe she pushed it back through the louver. "Keep it as a remembrance."

* * *

A week later Billy was leading a group of adults through a lunar rock garden. He stopped to observe one young woman bouncing in every conceivable direction. She was whooping and cheering oblivious to everyone else. He had seen excited visitors before, but their excitement usually wore off after the first half hour. Hers kept going.

"Miss, careful you don't over exert yourself." He looked through the bubble walls into her wild green eyes and bright smile and felt saddened for his inability to connect closer.

"I've never felt so frrreeeeeeeeeee!" She bounced up and down.

Reminds me of my first time out of my sterile containment, he thought.

Her orb stopped. "I'm sorry. You must be Billy! I'm Claire! You're supposed to teach me everything!" She started bouncing off nearby rocks.

Billy's eyes lit with excitement.

48

THE CIRCUS

by
Gail Harkins

In another hour dawn would break. Ella knew this with certainty, peering at the lightening sky around the edges of the trailer curtains. This same confidence propelled her serenely off the trapeze platform, through the air, and into the strong arms of her catcher. The challenge she was about to face required a leap of a different sort, and this time she was on her own. Butterflies filled her stomach. Today was the day. This was the moment. She rose, dressed quickly, and stepped into her parents' berth at the end of the trailer.

Her mother stirred. "Ella? Everything okay?"

"I'm fine, mom." She tiptoed in, kissed her cheek, and placed a note by the side of the bed. "Go back to sleep."

Ella grabbed her suitcase and stepped out into the cool morning air. Rosy golden tendrils wisped along the eastern sky. As she slipped past the cage containing the big cats, Simba twitched. She reached in and stroked his luxurious mane. "Sweet dreams, fella. I'm going to miss you."

Ella touched the incisor that dangled from a cord around her neck. "Mom said that when I left home, I should take this with me, so I'd never be far from the circus. You tell her I have it so she'll understand. Okay?" She stroked him one last time and then ran from the circus lot.

***

The frost made patterns on the windowpanes, but Ella gazed through them as she turned the problem over in her head. Confident she had the correct solution, she typed in her answer on her computer, hit *send,* and hoped for an *A.* Professor Rutledge was a stickler for detail, but Ella had a head for numbers.

Ella's ringtone sounded the trumpet of an elephant and her roommate grimaced.

"That's my dad," she explained nervously.

"How's my darlin' daughter faring in the alien world of rubes and marks?" the lilting male voice on the other end asked.

"I'm fine, Dad, and it's not really that different." Ella gazed out the window to the dried grass of the quad below and the gothic clock tower at its far side.

"We could debate that, darlin'. I'm calling because your mother's worried about you. She had a dream last night. You were fighting off numbers. Big nasty things with swords." He fibbed.

Ella laughed. Her roommate looked up from her books briefly. "Tell her not to worry. My classes are interesting, and I'm doing well. I enjoy accounting."

He sighed. "I'm glad to hear it, darlin'."

Ella knew something more was coming. "You didn't have to slip away in the night. You should have told us and said a proper goodbye. We're your family."

"I know, Daddy." Her voice was small and thin. "I didn't know how to tell you."

"You know you can always come home," he assured.

"I know, Daddy, but this is where I belong."

"The people you're with, are they treating you well? Are you safe? You're not staying out too late and walking back alone, are you?"

"Don't worry, Daddy. I'm safe, and the people are fine. My grades are good. I'm happy."

A lion roared in her dad's background.

"What's that?" Ella asked.

His voice perked up. "Roary's new beast. He added another lion to the ring. Simba's getting old. Oh! A couple of Québécois acrobats signed on last week, too. They have a good act. I put them in the center ring. The crowds really like them." He paused. "We miss you on the trapeze," he added wistfully.

"And I miss being there, but," she added firmly, "I really want to learn this. Later once I have my business degree and some experience, I can come back and help you take the company into the 21st century. Maybe take it public, invest in new equipment with the extra money, and do more marketing."

"Public? Tosh! We're doing fine. We just miss you."

She twined her hair round a finger. "I know, Daddy. Me too." Ella choked back a tear and then rallied. "I bought an ant farm. It arrived yesterday. It reminds me of home, at least a little." She tried to laugh. "Dad, I have to run to class now. I love you. Tell mom I love her too."

When she hung up she exhaled deeply and sat on her bed a moment regaining her sense of equilibrium.

"So that was your dad," her roommate said as she pushed her textbook aside.

Ella nodded.

"He's really over protective," her roommate continued. "After all it's not as if you ran off and joined the circus!"

49

THE LOST TREASURE

by
Sylvia Stein

It was a cold winter's night in the village of Betws-y-Coed in the country of Whales. There was a bit of rain that seemed to be increasing with the hours. I set out to investigate a lost treasure that was to be discovered in the very middle of a most confusing labyrinth. It could be anyone's demise when daring to find it. Now I am not one to give up on anything, so I set out with my two associates. We were determined to find what was hidden in the most complex labyrinth designed to trap everyone. This challenge was in the cards for me.

My name is Sebastian Cromwell, and I was asked by my father, James, to find the lost treasure. He had once found it, but the British government had taken it because there was some law that had not been followed. My father never seemed to have recovered after losing the treasure. This led to his declining health and eventual death. And now here I am today.

"Sebastian." One of my associates called out to me.

"Yes, Peter," I answered.

"Do you really think we will be able to find your father's lost treasure? Even if we do find it, we're never going to find our way out of the maze." Peter stated in a most pessimistic tone.

"Look, Peter," I added. "I assure both you and Jack that we will find the lost treasure, and we will make it out of the labyrinth."

After this reassurance to my crew, I checked on the carriage and horses. They were sturdy enough to make it to the outskirts where the maze would begin.

"Okay, this is it," I said as we arrived at the gigantic estate.

"Let's go," Jack said.

We began walking through the grassy entrance toward the large gate, but I was not prepared to see what was coming next. Inside this enormous labyrinth were multiple forks. It was then that I started to feel a sudden moment of panic.

What have I got myself into? What if I can't find the lost treasure? But just as I began to doubt, I felt a spirit beside me. "Father, is that you?"

No one answered, but I still felt like someone was helping me get to where I needed to go. As I walked along this very complex labyrinth, I went underneath what looked like a staircase that led to a bottom floor. Once I got there, I called out my two associates.

"Jack, Peter, come quickly!" I said in a very stern tone. As I called out to them, I overheard a large door slam.

"Yes, Sebastian!" Jack, my eager associate replied.

"Look what I have found." I said with a smile.

"No, could this really be?" Peter questioned what he saw.

"Yes, we have found the lost treasure, my father's treasure."

"But do you know how to get us out, Sebastian?" Peter asked. "I mean look at this place!"

"My father led me here," I smiled. "I feel his spirit with me everyday, and he will lead us out."

We looked at the box of treasure. I was amazed that we found the lost journals of my father's journey. "It took my father a very long time to find this treasure, and he had it ripped from him."

"Today is redemption day, Sebastian." Peter smiled.

"Yes, Sebastian," Jack agreed. "Your father can rest easy knowing his hard work lives on. What are you going to do with this treasure now?"

"I am going to honor my father's wishes by donating it to the people in the small village of Harmony. He always wanted them to receive it, but he never got the chance to share it."

My father led us out of the complicated labyrinth. We stepped out, and we knew that the lost treasure was now found. All was well again, just as it should be.

50

JAROB

by
Lynette White

As I stood alone in Nana's room, I couldn't bring myself to accept my dear sweet grandmother was dead. As the only granddaughter, I spent countless hours in here with Nana. My eyes settled on her jewelry box, and I picked through the necklaces and rings we shared over the years.

On the very bottom was a tattered carving that looked like some sort of beetle. The shape was vague, but the eight legs came to sharp points. I didn't remember ever seeing it and held up for a closer look.

"Well, aren't you an odd looking thing? Wonder which uncle made you or why Nana kept you?" I remarked.

I jumped as the door popped open, and my brother Jason and my cousin David stood in the doorway. "So this is where you disappeared to." Jason announced as he wandered in.

His eyes moved to the carving in my hand. "What you got?"

I held out the carving and a low whistle crossed his lips as he took it from me. "Ugly little sucker ain't it? Wonder where Nana got this poor thing?" He commented and opened his hand so it sat in the middle of his palm.

"So you gonna keep that, sis? Would fit right in with your wardrobe nowadays."

Jason disagreed with my fashion choices lately. I was going through an *everything-had-to-be-black* phase that started long before Nana's sudden death.

Before I could touch it, David grabbed it. David and I were not particularly close. He was a pretty boy with the attitude to match, so he annoyed me to death. "Huh, I think he is right, Lizzy."

I snatched it back from David. "Give me that."

A movement in the hall caught my attention. I pushed past them just in time to see my expensive iPod jump into the laundry shoot.

"Hey, give me that, you thief!"

Jason and David followed me. "What's up sis?"

"Something just stole my brand new iPod and jumped down the laundry shoot." I declared and started down the hallway.

I was almost to the staircase when David yelled, "That means you have to go into the basement, Lizzy."

I stopped dead in my tracks and started to tremble from head to foot. I was terrified of the basement. Jason sighed as he started toward me.

"Ch come on, sis, that was ten years ago. How many times do we have to tell you there was no one down there?"

My big brother put an arm around my shoulders and started to guide me down the staircase. "Come on, I will go with you. It was probably just a squirrel anyway."

"That knows how to use an iPod? Pretty smart squirrel." David quipped and followed.

Not long after we reached the basement, I spotted a tiny part of my earpiece cord near the wall. I thought it was broken, but discovered it was intact and the rest was on the other side of the wall.

I stumbled back, and when David and Jason joined me, I pointed a shaking finger at the wall. "It is in there," I whispered.

Their eyes followed my finger. "What the hell?" Jason muttered and yanked on the cord.

Whatever was on the other side yanked back and the cord disappeared. He stood up and started to search the wall. His hand found eight distinct holes.

"You got that bug thing, sis?"

I had slipped it into my pocket, so I handed it to him, and he pushed the legs into the holes.

The wall gave way to reveal a secret chamber and in the back of the chamber, clutching my iPod, was a little man no more than a foot high. I knew instantly he was the one I saw ten years previous.

"Who are you?" I choked.

"I am Jarob. I was Nana's memory keeper."

As I scanned the room, I found it was full of trinkets. I looked back at the little man. "You mean everything in here is linked to one of Nana's memories?"

He nodded.

"So, why the iPod? Nana never knew she had it?" Jason pressed.

Jarob suddenly looked so sad as he stepped forward and presented my iPod. "I was not going to keep it. I just wanted you to know I was here, so I was not forgotten."

51

TUNNEL OF DOOM

by
Janet Bond

"Hey, Tony. Want to go to Chicago for the fourth?" Jessie asked over the phone. "We can go to the carnival."

"Sure. Mind if I invite a couple of friends?"

They had been friends since first grade. "That would be great. Any friend of yours is a friend of mine. Let me know."

Tony called Brenda. "You want to go to the carnival tomorrow? It's with Jessie, and I want to prank her. Can't do it alone."

Brenda hesitated before replying. "Count me in. Jessie is a little full of herself. It'll be good to take her down a notch."

"Great. Gotta go. Need to invite Debra, too." Tony hung up.

After convincing Debra, Tony let Jessie know

everything was set.

The next morning Jessie picked up the three girls who were laughing and giggling as they got into the SUV.

"What's so funny?" Jesse asked.

Debra poked Brenda in the side with her elbow as they both tried to stop laughing.

"Nothing," Tony said. "Just talking about someone you don't know." Fresh laughter erupted from the backseat.

For most of the three-hour drive to Chicago, Tony was twisted around talking and laughing with Brenda and Debra. Jessie felt a little strange that the other girls were ignoring her, but she figured it was because she couldn't really look at them while she was driving.

When they reached the carnival, Tony suggested, "Let us out by the gate, and we'll get tickets while you park."

When Jessie got back to the gate, the girls were gone. Jessie stood in line, bought her own ticket, and started to explore the carnival. She played a few games, but was beginning to worry about Tony when she showed up.

"Sorry, Jessie. Didn't mean to ditch you. Debra had to use the bathroom."

"Where are they now?" Jesse asked.

"They were hungry, but I wanted to find you." The two girls played a few more games.

After they ate they found Debra and Brenda by the

bumper cards. The four girls spent the afternoon and evening together playing games, going on rides, and eating more junk food.

It was almost closing time, so there wasn't any line when they walked by the *Tunnel of Doom*. Brenda and Debra ran ahead disappearing into the tunnel's darkness.

"Come on, Jessie. It'll be fun," Tony said as she headed toward the entrance.

"I don't like all the fake blood. Let's do something else." Jesse pleaded.

"You're just scared. You can wait here if you want. I'm going in." Tony skipped off towards the entrance.

With a sigh Jessie followed slowly. When she entered Tony was gone.

"Tony. Where are you?" Jessie called. She only heard her own voice and the fake screams coming from the speakers. Jessie kept walking through the maze of mirrors and across a shifting floor that kept trying to make her fall. All the while she continued to call for Tony.

Jessie heard pounding and scraping sounds. Then she heard a scream. It was not like the fake ones. It was a real scream. "Tony!" She ran toward the scream calling out for Tony. Tears streaked her cheeks. She ran into several walls, but she kept running toward the screaming.

Then it stopped. Jessie stopped dead in her tracks, and looked around. "Tony!" There was no answer. Jesse rounded a corner and almost tripped over a body. She screamed when she saw it was Tony whose face was covered in blood.

Then she heard the laughing. Brenda and Debra stepped around the corner holding the bottle of fake blood.

Tony slapped Jessie on the leg, "Got you."

New tears streamed down Jessie's face as she ran out of the *Tunnel of Doom*.

The other girls joined Jessie outside. She was sitting on a bench hugging her knees.

"I thought you were my best friend," Jessie whimpered.

"It was just a prank," Tony laughed.

"I thought you were dead. I thought I could trust you."

"Hey, I'm sorry. It's just that you get on my nerves sometimes. You're so perfect. Come on, say it's all right." Tony responded dryly.

"But it's not all right. I don't know if it will ever be all right. I don't know if I'll ever be able to trust you again." Jesse's eyes were full of tears.

"Hey, I'm sorry. What else can I say?"

"I don't know if there is anything you can say." Jessie stood up and walked back to the car in silence.

The other girls followed her. They drove home in silence. When Jessie dropped them off, Tony said, "Come on, I said I was sorry."

Jessie drove off without saying a word.

CHAPTER 4

MASKS

52

MASQUERADE

by
Arlene Lagos

I've spent most of my life living on a small island just off the coast of Maine, a wonderful tourist attraction in the summer. My family and I owned a small grocery store where we took turns working. Growing up here had its pro's and con's. There were only fifteen kids even close to my age on the island. We attended school together every year at the little brick house at the bottom of the hill. In many ways it was great because we were all so close. So close that it was only a matter of time before we broke off into couples as our parents before us did. That's how I came to be with Roger.

We lived three houses down from each other and attended the same school. When that ended neither of us went to college. Instead, we became our parents—I worked the cash register at the store while he bussed tables at his father's Inn. My future was already written. I'd be engaged soon, then married, pregnant, and before I knew it, I'd be walking my own kids to the same school at the bottom of the hill. Except that I didn't want this life. For over two years, I'd seen my friends around me happily accept their fate, but something inside of me wanted out. I wanted out so bad that if I could run off the island without sinking, I would have done it. The problem wasn't Roger or even the island. The problem was that I wanted more. I wanted to see the world, meet new people, and experience new things.

I always loved summertime when the tourists would come to stay and talk about the big cities they lived in and all the experiences they had. I would eagerly listen to their stories, hanging on every word that dripped off their lips, and then go home at night and dream about someday being able to do the same.

Then one day, an opportunity knocked, and I answered. A traveling dance troupe out of NY was spending the weekend on the island. They were having a masquerade ball at the only place that had a big enough banquet room—The Wayside Inn—where Roger worked. I had often dreamed about auditioning for a dance troupe like this. Perhaps if I could sneak into the masquerade party in disguise and dance for them, maybe they would like me and take me with them. A foolish girl's dream, but I had to try.

Nighttime arrived quickly, and the music from the festival was singing through the trees as people lined up to enter the Inn. Nervously I stood there greeting people with a nod or a wave hoping nobody from the island would recognize me.

Everyone was dressed so colorfully, and the music was blaring—it brought the entire island to life. "This is what I want," I whispered to myself. I watched in awe as people broke off into groups and danced. I knew my time was coming, and I was ready. Then something strange happened. Everyone cleared the dance floor, and Roger walked up on stage with his father to make an announcement. The blood quickly drained from my face as I prayed they had not recognized me.

"Thank you all for coming to our beautiful island. We are happy to have you here. Our honored guest has arrived, and I believe she is ready to dance for you. Ladies and Gentlemen, Serena Ayer."

The spotlight came on, and I stood up in shock. My parents, neighbors, and friends all got on stage—their eyes fixed on me. My favorite song was playing—the one I'd been dancing to all these years. I pulled off my mask and let down my hair. Tears were rolling out of my mother's eyes almost in unison with mine. They had done this for me. They had brought them here—for me.

The crowd stood up and began clapping in unison cheering me on. This was my moment, and without further hesitation, I leapt onto the dance floor and danced for my life. My heart was exploding with freedom as I looked around the room staring at the friends and neighbors I spent my whole life with, the same people that pulled together—for one moment—to make one girl's impossible dream possible.

53

MEET THE GIRLFRIEND

by
Laura Stafford

Rich pulled into the lot and eyed the big white tent warily, and then he looked over at Janet.

He loved her, but he had no idea how his family was going to react to her thirty tattoos, six earrings in each ear, and black leather boots that she chose to wear to the *tea party*—a party his mother had arranged for their family in honor of his brother's acceptance to grad school.

In all honesty, despite how much fun drinking could be with Janet, sometimes Rich was embarrassed by her. She was willful and independent, and she spoke her mind without thought. She said and did what she wanted, and she made no apologies. It was a quality he loved and hated—a quality that he cherished and tolerated.

Janet chewed a long blue nail and stared at the

gathering of suits and sundresses.

"You sure you want to be here? We can go…if you want.. " He wanted to—or at least he wanted her to want to go—because then he would be indulging her instead of running from his shame of her.

"Of course not," she shrugged, nonchalantly. "I can't wait to meet your family!" She grinned, evilly.

Rich rolled his eyes because he knew that playful teasing grin.

"I'll be on my best behavior," Janet said, putting up her pointed fingers in some kind of mock salute.

He shook his head and they got out of the car together. Lingering slowly towards the shoreline where the Charleton family had set the rented party tent, he advised her on things to not say to his mother, actions his father wouldn't like, jokes his grandmother wouldn't appreciate, and words that were inappropriate anywhere in the crowd.

"Are you coaching me?" she laughed at him.

"Not at all," he lied.

Janet introduced herself, mingled, ate, drank, swore, and skipped rocks on the water with his cousins. She snorted when she laughed and told monstrous stories. Rich could see everyone staring at her.

Couldn't she put her good-girl mask on for just a while? There was no hiding the tattoos of fairies and skulls, of unicorns, and jailhouse style hearts. She couldn't change the blue streaks in her black hair or the line of holes that went up her right ear and down her left. But couldn't she just find a little decency to deal with this hierarchy he called his family?

Rich wanted to dive in the water and swim away from his family's criticism and ridicule, which he was sure to hear.

Until his dad clapped him on the back. "Hell of a girl you got there!" he told Rich.

"Your new girlfriend is so sweet!" his grandmother squeezed on his arm.

"You best be careful, Rich," his brother said punching. "I might just take that girl off to college with me!"

"She is a smart one," his mother agreed. "Did you know she has a degree in American Literature?"

She has a degree in American Lit? Suddenly Rich realized he knew very little about this girl. He had been dating Janet for two months and saying *I love you* for two weeks. But what did he love? Her? What she represented? Their time together?

He pulled her to the side by an elbow. His mother had planned this perfect party, and Rich didn't want her ruining it. "Why are you lying to my family?" he demanded.

"I'm not. What are you talking about?"

"American Lit?" he spat.

"Yeah? I have a degree in American Lit. I'm an English teacher. I leave to go to Ohio at the end of the summer to start working with the *Teach For America* program."

"Nuh-uh," Rich didn't know what to say. She was a partier, a drinker—how could she have intellect? He stumbled over words and found those with sentiment falling right out of his mouth.

"Huh," she said dryly. "You're so worried about your family judging me, how I'm going to act in front of them, and what they'll think about me. But you're the one who judges." Janet shook her head sadly. "You obviously don't think much of me if you think I'd lie to your family. I'm not the one pretending to be someone I'm not."

With that, Janet walked away. Rich waited for her to come back, but she didn't even ask him for a ride.

54

POSTCARDS FROM

PARADISE

by
Kristen Strassel

My skin burned. My mouth felt like I had drank sand. I peeled open my eyes, not sure where my crumpled body lay. All I could see was blue. Blue sky, blue water. This didn't look like Minneapolis.

"Help me! Please, get me out of here!" A woman's voice pleaded, snapping me to attention. We weren't in Minnesota, and something was very wrong.

I positioned my hands by my side to hoist myself up. Pain seared through my body. It was easy to ignore as I processed my surroundings—bodies, some bloody, some moving, some that would never move again. Broken luggage. Seats and pieces of twisted metal pierced the sand. In the distance smoke rose from the carcass of the plane that never meant to leave us here.

Palm trees swayed gently at the perimeter of the beach.

We'd crash landed in paradise.

"Help me! Please, somebody help me!" The lady's voice wailed continuously. I wanted to search for her, but first I needed to find my sister.

Not quite in one piece myself, I rummaged frantically through the mess piled around me. She had to be close by. After all we'd been sitting right next to each other on the plane.

"Oh, God, I'm gonna die! I don't want to die!"

"Where are you? Lady?" I needed her to shut up, so I could concentrate. Depending on what condition she was in, maybe she could help me find my sister.

"I'm under a propeller." I braced myself for the condition this lady could be in. The least I could do was help her, even though she would be of no help to me.

I scanned the rubble for recognizable plane parts and followed the whimpers. The poor lady was covered not only by a propeller but in her own blood. I pushed at the propeller, but it was much stronger than I was.

I sighed. "What do you want me to do? I can't move it."

"Pull me out if you can."

Terrified to hurt her anymore than she already was, I carefully tugged on her arms and remarkably was able to slide her abdomen and legs out from underneath the huge piece of machinery. She let out groans I didn't know a human was capable of making on the way out.

"Bless you."

"Have you seen my sister? I can't find her." I had to at least ask.

"There was another girl. She looked like you. I thought I was hallucinating."

"Really? Where was she?"

"They took her."

"What? What do you mean, they? Where?"

"The natives. Towards the trees."

I didn't even thank her before I stumbled off in the sand towards the palm trees. Who knows how long we'd been here, baking in the hot sun with no food and water. The trees became thicker, and I dodged the underbrush that scratched my face and my bruised shins.

A tattoo of drums became more rapid as I journeyed deeper into the jungle. Birds cawed, letting the natives know of my impending arrival.

An eerie peacefulness filled the clearing. Totem poles topped with real heads warned away intruders— but not me. These savages had my sister tied to a thick pole with firewood at her feet. I'd either arrived just in time to save her, or I'd given them an unexpectedly abundant feast.

"Stephanieeeeee!" My shrill cry echoed off the trees.

"Shannon! I'm so afraid! They're going to kill me! They already burned one of the stewardesses." She called between heaving sobs. There was no risk of her captors understanding what we said.

The natives, dressed only in elaborate face paint and

crude masks made of brightly colored feathers, halted their ceremonial dance at our exchange. All women—tall and spooky—surrounded me and came in close without touching me. I froze in the spot I stood in, knowing they could destroy me with very little effort.

One of the women grunted over her shoulder at another clan member. No one in the circle moved. Once a grunt came back in response, the woman nodded to the rest of the circle. Two of them picked me up by my arms and carried me to the middle of the circle, where a pole just like Stephanie's had been erected right beside her.

A native snapped rope back and forth in her hand, smiling at me.

55

FIRE ISLAND

by
Jot Russell

My husband continued to walk ahead of me, neither saying a word nor providing an occasion to slow down and take my hand. The beach was beautiful and desolate, spanning into an empty distance as far as the eye could see—a perfect retreat from the world that bustled just across Great South Bay. It must have been an hour since leaving Davis Park as we took Dune Walk across to Fire Island National Preserve. In an effort to connect with my husband, I struggled in solitude. This marriage that I agreed to drew in a terrible feeling of loneliness and confusion.

Even during lunch his disconnect showed through the flesh on his face. I must finish eating, and I must complete *his* journey. *Why can't he see this is our journey?* This is the same routine we faced each day in life— some even called it a marriage. But was it a marriage?

What is a marriage? Certainly it needed to be more than his goal to see us through this twenty-mile walk—just to brag to our friends.

I realized then that my life had become just another one of *his* goals—where we traveled, what we purchased, when we slept, and the time we woke. No, it wasn't a marriage. It was a mere mirage like the shadowy effect that projected off the hot sand. I tried to look toward *his* destination, but I still could not see it. I thought more about *his* goal of completion. Completion? I felt the weight of the sand lift from my feet as my own goals became clear. It was time I lived my own life. And the joyful, empowering feeling that surged through my being confirmed to me that my decision was just. It was so clear in thought that I knew—no one could argue me out of leaving my husband. I began to wonder if I would lose that moment in time and succumb to his words if I didn't force my position now.

I looked back up from the sand and opened my mouth to speak. To my surprise he had already halted his quest. He was standing there in the footprints—in the path that led to him. I paused six feet back. The late sun stretched the shadow that I cast upon him. *Can he sense my thoughts and look to reconcile his uncompassionate ways?* I found myself hoping so, but his expression was odd and troubling.

A bright flash of light from sun reflected off the object that he pulled from his back. I shifted my shadow to block the mirror's reflection, only to expose the jagged form of a large knife.

"I'm sorry it has to end like this," said my husband.

I screamed. The loud surf swallowed my cry that otherwise would carry it off into the distance toward ears of another soul. Without control over direction and concourse, I ran. My arms stretched out before me, as if they were needed to push others aside from my path. I willed them down to assist, but my method was erratic and inefficient. I could not control the desperate panting. It quickly drew what little energy I had left.

I chanced a look back and saw his simple steady pace gaining on me. As his hand reached out to grab my hair, I dodged left and plunged into the ocean. The knife came down and caught my pack. I screamed again from the resistance of my motion, but managed to expel my gear and make the final strides toward the first wave.

I welcomed the strong current that my father always warned me about. By the third crest his hand was upon my sandal. The wave hit and knocked us around. My foot found bottom and bounced me above for a breath. I was forced to dive under the next wave. He followed me beyond the breakers, and I could feel the current drawing us out to sea.

His apparent realization of the strong wave showed by his attempt to alter his course back toward the shore. His gear and boots exasperated his effort against the surge that slowly drew him under. Without form or thought, his instinct now controlled his effort to survive—but exhaustion sealed his fate.

I struggled to alter my own course—not directly against the current—but parallel to the beach as my father taught me. The ocean was angry and alive, but part of it was in my favor forcing my direction toward the east. Without sandals to bar my kicks, I patiently made it through the surf and back to shore.

56

FIRST VENICE,
SOON LONDON

by
Richard Bunning

Dear Mama and all the family,

(Aking mahal Momya at ang lahat ng mga pamilya,)

I hope this letter finds you all well. I love you all, and you must not worry about what I am going to tell you. It has been getting harder working on the ship, but I am happy because I've met a special man. I am sure that you would all approve of him. His name is Naeem. He comes from Ubari in Libya. He is very caring and responsible. He is three years older than me. I miss you all. I may be a very long time before I can visit Manila, but I will always send back money.

Naeem and I have decided to jump ship in Venice,

and try to start a new life in Europe. I have had to work for over twelve hours a day as a Stewardess. Naeem isn't supposed to be on board. He is one of a dozen or so on the ship without papers. With a crew of a thousand, it isn't hard for a stowaway to blend in. He got on in Tunis and has been aboard nearly as long as me. Naeem is known by everyone. He even works. He just doesn't get paid. I'm sure some of the senior crew must know that the work registers and employee names don't tally, but all the different nationalities and strange names help confuse things. I wonder if, when he leaves, he will even be missed, as another stowaway is already learning his job.

I do wonder if bad people, terrorists, could hide on board, camouflaged amongst the crew and passengers. We have to show badges for getting on and off ship, but it is possible to borrow them. No details, but we are going to both slip away when cargo is being loaded. I have a girlfriend that will cover for me. I helped her when she was sick for six weeks. I can swim if needed, but Naeem can't. He had never even seen the sea before the day he slipped aboard. His people are desert people. Naeem is terrified of water. That is funny because one of his duties is cleaning around the deck swimming pool. Remember how I told you about the pools on the boat? I still find the idea funny.

Now I must go and get our new passports. I've identified a young couple, the man is dark like Naeem, and the girl is near enough my skin tone that make-up can do the rest. They look very like us, and we can't afford to turn down such an opportunity. They don't know that their safe is now broken. I have no guilt, because they are both wicked people who tried to make me do sex with them. Don't worry, I can look after myself, and now I have Naeèm to protect me. We will use the passports to get through Italian customs, then I will change my disguise and hand in the passports just as though I'd found them dropped on the street. That way they will get back to those people.

I know you won't approve of what we are doing. Certainly you wouldn't approve of stealing passports, but I had to be honest with you about how much bad we are doing to prevent you from trying to interfere unless, of course, you wish us to go to prison. That couple came close to forcing me to give what I have given to no one, even to Naeem who loves me. Anyway, they won't suffer more than a bit of short-term worry.

We are already moored on the waterfront dock, and in the morning we cross it and enter Italy. We will have no luggage, but will just blend in with other day-trippers out for a few hours riding the gondolas on the canals and sightseeing. I will look for regular work, no more slaving over twenty cabins, twice a day. Naeem will find a job in construction, and we will keep our heads down. As soon as I can, I will be sending money home again. I beg you not to alert authorities to track us down. We just can't stay in the ship any longer. Naeem needs paid work, and we need to be together. I guess we will end up in London, where everyone says it is very easy to stay.

All my love, Anna

(Lahat ng aking pag-ibig, Anna)

57

WEDDING MASKS

by
Alli Vaughan

Mother's third marriage made my skin crawl. On the big day, she married Fred, her swag-bellied fiancé. He always smelled like the seat of a used car to me. The ceremony was bathed in purple hydrangeas and paper cups, blowing in the hot winds from Waterfront Park. I stood next to her as her only daughter. Holding her bouquet and wearing what I thought looked like a smile, my make-up was streaking off my face in the July sun.

As bad as the ceremony was, it wasn't nearly as uncomfortable as the reception. I guess after mother had two traditional weddings under her skirt, she decided anything goes for the third. The masquerade themed party in the long reception hall ushered in guests dressed in peacock plumes and silver sequins. After the ceremony, I'd wrapped my long purple dyed hair into a bun and strapped a slight bird's beak to my face. The mask itched, and my purple dress looked entirely too tight on my tall frame.

I stood near the punch bowl trying to avoid my crazy family members. One aunt after another made awkward conversation with me. Finally mother found me. She came to my side breathless and flushed in her pink swan outfit. "Oh, Emilia. Isn't this divine?" she asked, gripping my arm and staring at her large fluffy crowd of guests.

"Oh, yes," I said, trying to smile. My dress pinched, and I felt as if I might faint from the heat or from the boring conversation I'd been subjected to for the last hour.

"Don't worry, Emilia. You'll have your turn."

I froze at her words. I sincerely hoped not. The last person I wanted to end up like was my mother. Mother stood looking at me expectantly though, her hand on her thin hip. I began to stutter a response when I was interrupted.

A gallant hand swooped in at that moment to whisk me to the dance floor. "Third time is a charm," Uncle Eddie said, laughing as he spun me around. Even behind the silly mask, the crinkle of my uncle's eyes peeked through. I adored Uncle Eddie in that moment and not just because he was my only sane relative.

"You saved me, Uncle!"

"What do you mean?" he asked with a laugh.

"Mother was about to start in about me being the only single woman in the entire world at thirty." I shrugged and hung my head in exasperation.

"My sister," he said, as if that was enough of an explanation, and it kind of was.

We twirled among the other guests until my head spun, as we laughed and joked about my mother's unique taste. Uncle Eddie had a flash pan sense of humor, the kind that causes you to chortle out loud.

"Let's have a seat for a moment, Mellie," Uncle Eddie said, using his special name for me.

We sat at the table scooting a mountain of confetti and sparkles out of the way for our hands and drinks. "Fred doesn't look like he's having fun either," my uncle commented, pointing.

Fred wore a sparkly tux laced in black sequins, and a black mask covered the upper half of his portly cheeks. "No, he really doesn't."

"I don't think the man has cracked a smile the entire time I've known him." Uncle Eddie laughed.

"He'd better develop a sense of humor soon, marrying Mom."

Uncle frowned and grew still. *Uh-oh*, I thought. It was then I knew he wanted to talk about something serious. Uncle Eddie only grew silent for two things in his life—to eat Beef Wellington at Christmas and when he was working up the nerve to talk to his niece about something she didn't want to hear.

"Listen, Mellie," he started. *Here it comes*, I thought, debating how quickly I could make a run for it. "I wanted to tell you that you don't need to be afraid of this."

"Afraid?" My voice nearly cracked. "Me? Of what?"

"Look, your mom's your mom. You won't magically turn into her one day."

"Yeah, I know, Uncle Eddie. We could not be more different."

"Well, it's just that you seem to try to do everything in your power to be dramatically different from her. The hair is one thing," he said pulling on a purple lock, "but to travel around the world all of these years, and to not date at all, is another." Uncle Eddie was really serious.

He still hadn't cracked a joke yet.

I sighed. "Yeah, maybe you're right," I said, drinking my pink punch. Uncle Eddie looked at me a little shocked. It wasn't the reaction he was expecting, I guess.

"I love you, Mellie."

"I love you too, Uncle Eddie."

A dark haired man walked by smiling my way. Uncle leaned in and whispered, "You never know when fate will come your way."

"Care to dance?" I heard from the handsome stranger.

"I'd love to," I heard myself saying.

58

THE GUARDIAN
OF THE LAKE

by
Harry Alexiou

Lord Gorath wore the Mask of Superiority, and he wore it with pride as had the generations of Defender Vorkans before him. He lifted the mask and steadied the black stallion as it shook its mane repeatedly. The low sunlight bounced off the shimmering lake, an indication to him that the time to fight grew ever closer. The land beyond the lake had never been conquered by his people, but his carefully crafted plan promised success. The mask would see to it. Never before had the Vorkans endeavoured to invade other people. Their defences were impregnable and legendary for it. But the many years of stagnation had created a desire for something else in each new generation—a desire for new lands, more fertile perhaps. Shardan, son of

Gorath, sat proud upon his steed but was hesitant as they neared the edge of the vast expanse of water.

"My son," Lord Gorath raised his spear and pointed, "look across the waters and tell me what you see."

Shardan studied the far off land laid out before the white-capped mountains before answering. "My Lord, I see a land covered in lush green vegetation and most probably more game than we could eat in a millennium!"

Father and son enjoyed a raucous laugh. Although Shardan laughed, he was as close to the water's edge as he dared, and he sensed the presence of the beast. The age-old tales surrounding the Guardian of the Lake had been forgotten, and the tribe was happy in their ignorance. He would not allow his recent encounter to sour the mood especially with so much at stake. The water rippled slightly in the distance, and Shardan drew in a sharp breath troubling his horse as it backed up a step.

"You seem full of the woes of the whole of Vorkania, my son. Something troubles you?"

"Fear not My Lord, my thoughts are only for a successful campaign across the water to the Northern shores. The time nears does it not?"

"Indeed, it does my boy—one more of the setting sun and we begin our journey. When the lake is as still as a freshly slain Dervilbuck and the light of the day is no more, then we launch north with one hundred water vessels and claim the new lands. Victory will be ours!"

Shardan clenched his fist and joined his father in a premature victory salute. To speak of his recent experience would be to poison the air and invite an almighty rebuff from his father. To be branded a coward would only end in an untimely death for him. Cowardice would not be tolerated. No, he would not talk of it. He would grit his teeth and face the creature when the time came. He was sure it would.

Lord Gorath slipped the mask back on, and it gently formed itself to his features—a perfect fit for those eligible. A few of the tribes-people had foolishly worn the mask only to be consumed with madness until the body withered, and they died a slow painful death.

As the riders turned and headed back to Vorkania, the Guardian of the Lake lifted its head silently from the water and fixed its gaze upon them. He too, was ready for the campaign.

59

MY TERRIBLE TUX

by
Oliver Dolan

The cold crisp ocean water has always seemed to put my mind at ease. No one can talk to me while I'm submerged. They may see me down here swimming awkwardly, but they haven't the slightest clue of what's going on between my ears.

My mind, swaying with the refreshing water, suddenly drifts from happy to miserable thoughts. I think about where my life is going, the girl I once thought I'd spend the rest of my life with, and what the meaning of life is.

I break the surface, take a deep breath, and glance back up towards the beach to see Joyce and her parents wave and fake smiles, so I return the favor.

Joyce and I spent a lot of time planning this getaway to the shore. We've had some difficulties lately, and we decided it'd be good for us to get away. After college we put together our life savings and opened a nice little restaurant called *Relish and Rejoice*. It was a pretty dumb idea looking back, as we'd only known one another for a little over a year and mistakenly mixed business with pleasure.

The restaurant has been pretty successful, and we're close to turning it into a nationwide chain. I haven't proposed yet—and don't know if I ever will—because as our business has gotten better, our relationship has gotten worse. The energetic blue-eyed beauty I met in college has become cold and short with me, although her looks still make my heart skip a beat.

After a particularly terrible argument one night a few weeks ago, she told me she had invited her parents to join us at the beach. I'd never met them before and hadn't even seen a picture. All she ever said about them was how much money they had, though we never saw any of those dollars.

I trudge out of the water, through the sand, and up to our spot on the beach. I help Joyce and her parents take down the umbrella and shake sand off the towels. As I'm doing so, I look over one of the towels and deep into her father's eyes. As he stares harshly back into mine, an eerie feeling shoots through my body. He looks nothing like her, and come to think of it, neither does her mom.

"Scott, honey," Joyce says, interrupting my train of thought.

"Mom and dad got the four of us reservations for

dinner tonight on one of the big ships!"

"Supposedly their seafood is marvelous!" Chimes in her mother.

"I ordered you a tuxedo through the hotel. It should be in our room soon," explains Joyce.

"Sounds good babe!" I reply energetically.

We begin walking back toward our hotel, and I notice that her father has been very quiet—hardly saying a word. He didn't shake my hand when we met. And at this point I don't really know what to think about him.

Joyce and I break off from her parents and head to our room. She pours me a glass of scotch and a glass of red for herself. I knock it back—the scotch. She pours me one after the other, only taking a sip of red for each glass I inhale. My head becomes cloudy, and I step outside for a smoke. I look off the balcony at the sunset. My body is warm, and my mind is cloudy from the scotch. Joyce opens the door and smiles at me.

"I'm running over to my parent's room to get ready, I hadn't realized how late it's gotten. Dad's going to come over and get ready with you."

"Okay, sounds good, see you soon."

I stub out my cigarette, head back inside, pound some more scotch, and put my tuxedo on. I like the way I look in the mirror, and feel fairly confident that Joyce and I will work out our differences and live happily ever after. I think I hear the door creak open, but convince myself that if it was her dad, he'd knock. I brush my shoulders and bend down to tie my shoes.

Suddenly I hear footsteps from behind me and turn to find Joyce's father. He grabs my throat, and I feel a blade thrust through my lower back. He turns me toward the mirror, and I see blood stain my crisp tuxedo shirt. He stares me down through a ski mask and whispers in my ear as blood fills my mouth and my vision goes blurry.

"I'm not her dad, you idiot. I'm her lover. Die slow, Scotty boy."

LAGO LANDER
ON MARS

by
H. M. Schuldt

Each of the nine Landers brought a new species to Mars. All was well with Tungsten's Lago Lander. It began to touch down on the cold planet. Several foxes were anxious to get out.

Tungsten scanned the controls from Florida where she gladly accepted a Mars mission last year in 2018. As a director she watched over one of the nine Landers—the Lago Lander. Her team cheered as it landed safely on the surface of Mars.

Making the trip from Earth in less than one year, the Lago Lander was the first in this mission to touch down on September 20, 2019, in Mars's biggest crater, the Hellas Planitia. Tungsten held fast to the two main goals of the Lago Lander—to check on Curiosity's drill sight,

Uplison, and to observe the release of a new species in a new permanent residency.

A golden light of late afternoon sun gave the air a beautiful glow of false warmth. Tungsten would wait all night, if she had to, for the other eight Landers to touch down. When the time was right, she released a Lago Air Scope, the LAS, to gather data in the surrounding area and to search for Curiosity.

Flying close to the ground, Tungsten's team marveled by video surveillance when they found the Flora Rover, a vehicle from the 2016 mission. The Flora Rover had brought Arctic seeds to start vegetation on Mars. Half of the people on Earth doubted such a mission could be accomplished. Moving past desire, the other half held onto hope. The LAS gave proof to the beauty in the midst of a chill—Purple Saxifrage, Arctic Moss, and grasses covered the entire crater.

Three years ago plant life took hold in the spring on Mars. It grew heartily in the summer and lasted throughout the winter. The Flora Rover had also sent out numerous heaters throughout the crater that helped to change the atmosphere in a limited area by achieving balanced and habitable conditions. The crater now held a lake at the bottom, the only source of drinkable water chemically balanced for what was about to come out of the nine Landers.

The LAS traveled past man-made tunnels from the 2013 mission. It traveled for some time toward a natural cave. As they went into the cave, the temperatures rose the deeper they went into the crust as if they were traveling down from a mountain toward sea level. Miles and miles they traveled until they were greeted by Curiosity.

Curiosity had been resting from dust storms while waiting for the LAS to arrive. Traveling down further into the cave, Curiosity led the LAS toward the recent discovery of a clay pot. The LAS was to remove and examine any contents. Tungsten's team took sight of what everyone on Earth had been talking about. There in the Uplison Cave, the pot looked much like an urn. A camera zoomed in on the engraving. It read:

In Memory of
Alexandra Caroline Marie Charlotte Louise Julia
(1844-1925)

The LAS held up the natural looking urn. Someone on Tungsten's team recalled that Alexandra was the wife and queen-empress consort of King Edward VII of the United Kingdom and the British Dominions, Emperor of India. How did this urn end up on Mars? The LAS was about to reach inside and take out the contents— but it shattered—breaking into a million pieces.

Disappointed at first, the Tungsten team felt a great failure. For a moment she regretted sending the LAS into the cave for such an important task—a task that several others insisted was not for her. The camera scanned down showing an item among the ash and rubble. Something seemed to be rolled up. The LAS reached out a probe, discovering a piece of paper, brownish with silver specks. A small fan blew away a mask of dust. A probe took hold of one edge, slowly opening up the item. It appeared to be paper. Tungsten and her team were speechless when they saw the word—*Hershey's*.

"Quick, Higgs. File a photo. Get me a year when it was made," Tungsten said.

The LAS slowly turned over the paper, revealing a simple sketch and the title, *Vela*. Tungsten gave Nix directions. "Nix, pull up the constellation, Vela."

Nix located a ship constellation on the screen. It matched the sketch on the backside of the wrapper. On another screen, Higgs showed the exact same wrapper from the Uplison Cave. They noticed the date of the milk chocolate bar wrapper—*1925*.

Tungsten sent the LAS back to the Hellas Crater as her team agreed not to leak any news until further instructions. They were not going to be accused of any hoax. Flying over the crater edge, it began to soar down. Her team saw that the other eight Landers had released a historical delivery.

The LAS flew to watch the Lago Lander open its doors. The time had come. Heating mirrors rotated. Out came twelve Artic foxes, immediately leaving the Lago burrow, stepping on new ground. Tungsten's team sat in silence while they viewed a new world, a historical moment. Five Landers released young caribou, Arctic hare, Arctic ground squirrels, lemmings, and musk oxen as they explored a new life. Three fowl Landers sent out snow geese, Pacific golden plover, and snowy owls.

"Tungsten," said Higgs, "you're never going to believe it. Someone from Vela must have brought the wrapper to Mars in 1925."

"Don't tell anyone yet," said Tungsten. "Soon we will be in a race to get to Vela. The Velians have already been to Earth and stole the Queen's ashes. They might even be living among us today—in disguise."

61

OBSESSION

by
Randy Dutton

Khayyam's poetic phrase was my obsession since high school:

> *A jug of wine,*
> *a loaf of bread,*
> *and thou singing beside me*
> *in the wilderness.*

Ten years ago I heard the question, "If you could have three things on a desert island, what would you desire?" It was meant more as a school newspaper icebreaker than an obsessive challenge. Mulling the question, my infatuation grew—the infatuation of a young beautiful pop singer who everyone adores. She is alone with me. In my dreams romance did blossom.

The warm breeze flows over my tanned shirtless body. Sitting in the sand with an ocean-smoothed rock behind me, I take in the incredible view. The surf breaking over the reef is illuminated by incalculable stars.

I'm content here.

I roll my head to gaze upon her lithe body curled up on a palm frond mat. The campfire embers are cold on the beach. She's sleeping now. That's good. What a night we had, so long and active.

I tip my lightened champagne bottle toward her just meters away. "To you Hēbē, goddess of youth!"

I gulp the remains and jam the bottle into the black sand next to the other empties.

"It wasn't easy making you mine." I close my eyes and recall what I've done.

If not for my planning, what would a twenty-one year old songstress have seen in a twenty-nine year old skinny computer geek like me? Making this happen seems like a fantastic impossible adventure. The planning took effort and skill. I read of her pending singing tour. I hacked and manipulated itineraries along with aircraft electronics, manifests, and personnel files. It took months to spoof a tour organizer's identity and get her on that plane with no one else but me. I even ensured the flight crew was too old to compete.

I flip open my laptop and the screen lights up with paparazzi images of my companion.

You're so entrancing in these photos, so beautiful and strong.

I activate software to automatically reposition the portable satellite transceiver next to me. Soon I'm perusing a news account of the missing diva. Reuters reports:

Hēbē and Five Others
Lost at Sea During USO Tour

I read further:

...radio contact lost...
...transponder malfunction...
...South Pacific search called off after 10 days...
...world mourns....

I've got to make this right. Last week's been like hell for both of us. What was I thinking? She's so beautiful when painted up, so bland when she's not. Every day her pale face is sunburnt, and her eyes are dark from tears. How was I to know her entourage masked her weaknesses? For her everything is too dirty, too hot, or too cold. She can't stand the bugs or what might be in the water. She hates seafood. Isolation scares her. We have apparently nothing in common. She calls me her hero for pulling her out of the sinking plane, but when she seeks my comfort, there's no joy—only tears. Even her voice now grates on me—so powerful in concert but so squeaky without electronic enhancement. That makes the petty nagging even more intolerable. I'd rather be alone.

I glance to my left. If a search plane ventures five hundred miles south of the intended flight path, these broken palm trees and the shallow trench leading to the lagoon are a giveaway. Starlight glints off the few feet of cargo plane tail still above the tide. I only meant to force the plane off course to land on the abandoned WWII airstrip. I didn't mean for others to die.

I tap my keyboard linking to websites set up in Hēbē's memory. Hours later, I'm exhausted from posting anonymous reports of sightings and tips—all pointing to this deserted island.

Dawn's breaking.

I stash the electronics in one of the many waterproof bags I had manifested onto the flight, and I hike into the island's interior. I had secretly removed the electronics and the sleeping pills from the sunken plane after the crash. I connect the ruggedized laptop to a solar panel wired to a battery and transformer. For today, I pull out three cans of food and another bottle of wine.

I'm soon back at camp. "Good. You're still sleeping off the pills I slipped into your dinner."

In the early light, I wade into the lagoon and leave my netted bag carrying today's provisions underwater near the wreck.

After you wake, I'll retrieve them to maintain my illusion.

I lay down next to her to rest.

Five days tops and sighting rumors should force a redirected search. Then I'm free—of you!

THE GOOD HUMOR MAN

by
Gail Harkins

"I was saved by an ice cream truck." The incongruity wasn't lost on Natalie, a perpetual dieter, as she told the story to her granddaughter fifty years later. "I was at the beach—waiting in line for a cherry Rocket Pop—when sirens wailed and everybody started screaming and running away from the water. Everything was a blur until later when I found myself clinging to that truck floating in the Pacific Ocean."

* * *

After the waves subsided, Natalie's first memory was being cold, shivering in her wet clothes, and smelling the sweet stench of diesel fuel. The thunk of logs jostling against one another and gulls crying from above finally penetrated her foggy mind. Slowly she opened her eyes.

She was lying on an ice cream truck drifting in a sea of debris. Pulling herself higher onto the truck, she looked shoreward. Nothing remained of the seaside town. The realization that she was alone—alive but alone—formed a weight in her heart. Cold tendrils of fear radiated outward, numbing her to the devastation, but she slowly focused her intent upon one thing—surviving.

A fire engine red shipping container floated some hundred yards away, a bright spot in the sea of broken homes, crushed boats, and shattered dreams. Sometime that afternoon, it sank beneath the water.

This truck's sinking too, Natalie realized. *I've got to find a safer place.* She scanned the water for the thousandth time. *There must be something else big enough to support me.*

Blown by the wind the truck was approaching a flat spot on the water. *An oil slick? No, a dock... a floating dock!* She squinted her eyes. Relief flooded her body. *Is that...is somebody on it?* Natalie balanced precariously on the rear doors of the bobbing truck—yelling and waving.

He sees me!

When the dock finally drifted closer, Natalie caught the end of the rope he tossed. Together they pulled and closed the distance.

"Jump!" encouraged the man.

Natalie jumped.

"Anything in the truck?" he asked as she picked herself up off the deck. The hand he extended was large and beefy.

"Probably. I was afraid opening a door would sink it…"

"Now's the time to find out. Can you catch?" She tilted her head in puzzlement as he jumped back to the truck. He opened the cargo door. "If I throw you ice cream containers, can you catch them?"

"Sure."

"Name's Matt, by the way," he added, grinning.

"Natalie," she grinned back.

They feasted on ice cream that night and often in the ensuing years.

* * *

Natalie smiled reminiscing. "During those terrible days, your grandpa never lost his head. He had a mental list of what to salvage and how to use it. He was prepared, and that helped him keep his humor even when I was despairing."

"How were you rescued, Grandma?" Linda prompted leaning forward.

Natalie sighed. "After a couple days, the low clouds lifted, and we saw planes and helicopters—first military surveying the damage, then news crews from Seattle and Portland. I had a mirror in my purse. Yes, I'd slung my purse across my shoulder and managed to keep it throughout the ordeal. Matt signaled SOS. Eventually a pilot spotted us and alerted the Coast Guard which sent a rescue crew."

"And then you married Grandpa?"

"Not exactly. He was afraid—we both were—that our love was just a survivor's reaction—an adrenalin relationship. So we each rebuilt our lives but kept in touch. I went back to the ballet and shared the trials and tribulations of being a young ballerina with him. He was always supportive, but he didn't share much of his life. About a year later, we arranged to meet. He told me then that he had been a prisoner on a work detail when the tsunami struck. Originally he had planned to disappear and assume a new identity, but after our experience together, he couldn't do that. He told me he had fallen in love on that floating dock. It changed him. Amidst the wreckage, he began to understand what was important—sharing, helping others, and love. When we were rescued, he turned himself in."

A cherry Rocket Pop in a gnarled hand appeared to Natalie's left.

"For you, my dear." Matt's blue eyes softened as he looked at his wife and granddaughter. "We'd been spared, Linda. I realized it was time to make my life count. I just had to figure out how."

THE ENGAGEMENT PARTY

by
Sylvia Stein

As Sabrina awoke that morning, she was so happy. You see, after all these months of planning and waiting to be with the man of her dreams, the moment had arrived. Well, granted it was just her engagement party, but all in all, they both agreed to keep their engagement short. She smiled as she brushed her hair and stared at herself in the mirror. She was a bit distracted by her own thoughts, and she did not notice that her fiance had walked in the door.

"Oh, hey, Mitchell," said an excited Sabrina as she embraced him.

He smiled at her tenderly and then gave her a brief kiss. "Well, all I can say is you are looking more precious than ever!"

Sabrina was just so in love with Mitchell Anderson. He had been her one true love all through high school and throughout their time away at college. Sabrina had pursued her career at law school and was going to be a Defense Attorney. Meanwhile Mitchell was the CEO of his own investment company. Everyone that knew Sabrina and Mitchell could not be happier.

All preparations for the big engagement party were being handled. There seemed to be a mystery looming over the waterfront property, the location where the party was to be held. You see, a mystery person was hiding in the back of a cabin and decided to emerge secretly while the party planners and caterers were setting up.

Back in Sabrina's room, she noticed how quiet Mitchell seemed to be. It was one of the many things that she knew about her fiance. Anytime something was on his mind, his greenish eyes would become a bit gray.

"Babe," she said in a worrisome tone. Then continued, "Is something the matter?"

He quickly reassured her, "Oh, no, my darling." Then with a big smile added, "I am just so happy, and my adrenaline is running high."

"Oh, well, I am too," she answered and then embraced him with a big kiss.

Sabrina did not know that for the longest time Mitchell had been hiding a big secret—one that he hoped Sabrina would never learn. It was regarding his mother. This whole time Sabrina thought his beloved mother had passed away due to a terrible illness. Sadly that was not true.

The poor woman was being held in the Anderson's waterfront cabin. She had a few people that tended to her. She seemed to always want to be covered up in a masquerade mask. Mitchell's mother Clara had developed a mental disorder while Mitchell was growing up. As time went on she only got worse and worse. Therefore Mitchell's father decided, for the sake of the family name, he would say that she had passed on. But only a few knew the truth. It became harder and harder to keep her institutionalized. Mitchell pleaded with his father to let her stay at the cabin. That way from time to time, he could stop in and visit her.

At first his father thought that it was out of the question, but since he still loved Clara, he decided to let her be taken to the cabin. He made sure several guards surrounded her, and he saw to it that she had around the clock nurses. It was a painful journey for all of them— most of all for Mitchell who had to keep the secret from his beloved Sabrina. It had been more than five years now, and it was too late to turn back. All Mitchell could ask for is that everything would turn out for the evening events.

That evening all the guests arrived and greeted both of them.

"Oh, my dear," said Mr. Powell. "You look amazing!"

"Daddy, you would say that," said a beaming Sabrina.

"Oh, my baby," called out her mother.

"Oh, mom, please do not cry," she stated. After all this is only the engagement party!"

About an hour after all the guests were gathered by the nice marina near the waterfront property, Mitchell's father made preparations to give a toast to the happy couple.

"Well, good evening everyone," he said proudly. "I am so glad you could make it to Mitch and Sabrina Powell's engagement party. Let us give a toast to my son and his lovely fiancé." He paused. "Oh, gosh," he said trying not to get choked up. "These two have known each other since they were kids growing up here in Ann Harbor in the state of Michigan. I have known Sabrina's parents for a long time, and they are my very best friends."

As he continued, a dark figure with a masquerade mask was looming in the night. The figure moved into the midst of the party.

"Did someone forget to invite me?" said what appeared to be a woman.

Suddenly Mitchell's father began to look pale.

"Oh my, your father looks like he has seen a ghost," Sabrina said in a panicked tone.

"Mitchell! Mitchell!" called out the uninvited Clara in a hysterical cry.

All of a sudden, Mitchell's father called out to the guards to escort Clara back to the cabin.

"Mitchell," said a more concerned Sabrina. "Why is she calling you?"

"Sabrina, I am so sorry," he said. "This woman is my mother."

"I thought your mother died years ago," Sabrina said with a distraught look.

"Sabrina, we have to talk," he said in a more serious tone. Then they walked out as Sabrina's parents walked toward John Anderson to demand answers. All the guests were asked to leave due to a family matter.

Back at the cabin, Clara sat with her masquerade mask and pretended to dance the night away as Mitchell's father sadly looked on.

"Well, that was some *engagement party,*" said a few of the guests as they walked out.

64

HOMECOMING

by
Lynette White

Britney kicks a rock into the breakers. She curses herself for coming back. The note says:

Meet me at our beach at 10:00

There is no more of OUR anything. He made that perfectly clear one year ago when he left me in a crumpled heap on this very beach.

"I am leaving in the morning for Europe," he had said.

To this very moment those words cause a pain that refuses to be vanquished. She has simply learned to live with it. She did not deserve to be abandoned— not like that.

* * *

The pain he inflicted was so crippling she wanted to die that night. Instead she had finally made her way home. She still does not know what she did to deserve that from him.

The only correspondence from him since that night was a single postcard from Greece stating he was fine. She was not to worry about him. The first six months, she wasted hours on this cursed beach staring out at the sea. One minute she silently pleaded for him to be on the next boat. The next minute she hoped he endured a painful death. Her best friend, Jasmine, finally convinced her to stop torturing herself. That was when she made the vow to never return to this beach again.

She had started to move on until last week an acquaintance remarked that she saw someone who looked just like Derrick at one of his old haunts. To make matters worse, Jasmine had been acting like she had a secret she was dying to tell but forced herself to hold her tongue.

Tonight the note was under Brittany's door when she got home from work. She battled with herself for the next two hours before she concluded she had to know who could do something this cruel to her.

* * *

A movement catches her attention. A man is coming toward her wearing a stupid black Halloween cape. He is looking down at the ground, so his face is hidden under the brim of a stylish black hat. His movements do not dictate harm. In fact they are cautious and hesitant as if he debates whether or not to approach her. As she focuses on him, she sees the white pants and catches a glimpse of the pink shirt. She loves to see him in those clothes, but few people know that.

What kind of sick cruel joke is this? Why would someone intentionally rip open wounds that are just starting to heal? He stops a safe distance away.

"You came." He greets her.

She sucks in her breath at the sound of his voice. "No," she whispers.

He looks up, and she cannot believe she is looking into those intense green eyes again. A torrent of emotion rushes through her in an instant, and she is frozen.

"Hello, Brit." He says and cautiously steps forward.

"Derrick," she chokes out. "What are you doing here?"

He unties the cape and lets it drop into the sand. *Dear God, he is gorgeous in his pink shirt, white pants, and*

European tan. Then he smiles, and there are those dimples she adores.

"I am here because I know this is where I belong, Brit. I have been surrounded by beautiful women on exotic beaches only to realize I never felt more alone in my entire life. It took me a year to realize there is only one beach I want to be on and only one woman who is truly beautiful to me."

He moves closer.

"I was prepared to accept I missed my chance when I met with Jasmine last week. She assured me you had not moved on, but she made sure I understood how much pain I caused you."

He reaches up and touches her face.

"I am so sorry, Brit. I never meant to hurt you like that. I was too stupid to see I had the most precious woman any man could ask for. I know this is more than I deserve, but I am asking for a second chance. I realize now how much I cherish you, and I will never forget that again. I love you, Britney Owens."

All that emotion explodes, and she collapses into his arms in tears. He has no idea if they are tears of joy, but he will not worry about that until they stop. He pulls her close to comfort her while he awaits his fate.

65

BOCA GRANDE KEY

by
Janet Bond

They were on an annual sailing trip down to the Florida Keys. Cami loved these yearly trips with her older brother. It made her feel like they were still a family even though Kaleb had moved out of the house.

Day three found them in Key West, restocking the small galley of their sailboat. They had never been this far and were excited to see new sights. In the morning they set sail.

"Where to, bro?" asked Cami.

"West. The Key West National Wildlife Refuge is beautiful."

Kaleb was right. Cami lay on the deck, watching the lush green keys go by.

"Kaleb, look. Over there." Cami pointed where a white beach stretched out from a rugged tree covered shoreline. "Boca Grande Key. Isn't it beautiful?"

"Sure is. Let's drop anchor and go visit."

"We can't. It's a wildlife refuge."

"We haven't seen anyone all day. With all the cut backs, I bet they don't even have one ranger patrolling."

Cami tried to protest but soon gave up. She knew that once Kaleb had made a decision, it was hard to change his mind.

They dropped anchor. Cami packed some food and water for lunch. The trip to the small beach was rough. The dingy was rocking side to side. Waves came over the side and started filling in. Kaleb tried to keep the waves to the back of the boat, but each wave turned them again.

"Rocks!" Cami yelled, and Kaleb fought to keep the dingy off the rocks. Exhausted they finally gave themselves to the waves, which mercifully drove them to the white sands of the beach. They pulled the dingy up onto the beach, took off their life jackets, and then collapsed.

Cami looked up and saw at the top of the hill a strange looking man. She sat up. He was standing there half hidden by bushes. He was tall and pale looking—his hair was white. He held branches of some kind in his hands.

Cami's body shook as she pointed at him. "Kaleb, up there." Kaleb rolled over and looked where she was pointing.

"I don't see anything."

"It was a man. He was staring at us."

"Come on, Cami. You know, there's no one out here but us."

They rested for a while, and Cami tried to convince herself that Kaleb was right. After they ate a sandwich, Kaleb said, "Let's go explore this island. We almost died getting here."

"I don't know, Kaleb. This island looks creepy. Let's go back to the boat and leave," suggested Cami. But when Kaleb started walking up the beach towards the trees, Cami followed. They began to hear strange sounds—hollowing, screeching and squawking—which got louder and louder.

"You're not going to let a little noise scare you?" asked Kaleb.

Cami wanted to answer *yes* and run away, but she didn't want to let her brother see her scared. She managed to shake her head *no,* and she walked toward the trees.

After a hundred feet, the trees ended in an inland marsh. Cami screamed and wrapped her arms around Kaleb when she saw the man again. He was standing in the water of the marsh. He was naked except for a big mask made from woven grass that he held in front of his face. Through the mask Cami could still see his eyes glowing red.

The man pointed towards the beach. As Cami and Kaleb stood there, he turned and walked into the water. Kaleb broke away from Cami and followed him.

"No, Kaleb! You can't swim!" Cami yelled.

"Hey! Who are you? What's your name?" Kaleb called after him.

The man kept walking. Kaleb reached out to stop him. When his hand touched the man's shoulder, his fingers went through. The man stopped and turned toward Kaleb. With the mask still in front of his face, he pointed down into the water with his other hand.

Kaleb was in shock when he realized that the water was ten feet deep and he was standing on top. He looked through crystal clear water and saw the remains of a small boat. Kaleb suddenly became worried when four human skeletons came into focus sitting at the bottom.

Cami went running and then swam towards her brother. Kaleb splashed as he began to sink. He tried to scream, but water rushed into his mouth. He flailed in the water and was caught in a panic. Cami finally reached him and somehow managed to pull him back to shallow water.

The ghost stood on the water and pointed for them to stay on the beach. But Cami didn't need his prompting. She pulled Kaleb behind her and never looked back while the ghost moved through the trees deep into the island.

MASKS

PART TWO

AFTERWORD

$\mathcal{A}$FTERWORD

by

Arlene Lagos

* * *

WAKING

My cousin Holly was kidnapped many years ago. She was only ten years old. I was eighteen at the time, and it was the most horrifying thing I had ever witnessed. For months, family, friends, and neighbors posted amber alerts looking for her. Eventually we came to believe she might have been murdered and left somewhere to die. Everyone combed the woods looking for her body— hoping they'd find her alive—but knowing that they probably wouldn't. I remember thinking to myself, *What happens to her soul if they don't find her body? Will she go to heaven?* I had the worst nightmares wondering what would happen to her if she didn't have a proper burial. I wanted to run and go find her myself. I prayed everyday that they would find her alive, and if not, at least that they would find her. Eventually they did find her body. Still to this day, it is very hard for all of us, but I take comfort in knowing that she is in heaven now, and her soul is at peace. RIP Holly Piiarainen. 1/19/83-8/5/93

***

THE STORM GODDESS

I have very vivid dreams, and sometimes they are so vivid I wonder if they actually happened. Sometimes I feel as though my dreams are trying to tell me something—something hidden way back in my subconscious that I need to bring to the front. I also find that in my dreams, I dream often about time running out, and then usually my alarm goes off—as if I knew it would.

***

MASQUERADE

The setting of this story was inspired by a real place called Monhegan Island, just off the coast of Maine. Good friends of ours live there, and my husband and I actually eloped on that very island. I remember wondering what it would be like to live on such a tiny island, so far away from the hustle and bustle of everyday life. The thought frightened me. I also remember wondering if getting married would mean the end of my identity—as I knew it. *Could I still be me once he and I become we?* Nine years later we are still happily married, and I'm proud to say I've never had to masquerade as anyone but myself. I am still me. And we are still we.

* * *

REFLECTIONS

I wrote this to highlight Freud's theory of the Id, Ego, and the Superego and the roles they play in our everyday lives. In the story, the character's first instinct is to act on impulse and rage without really thinking it through. When she is brought to the house of mirrors, she is tested by her own mind. The Id telling her to fight, the Superego telling her to let it go, and her Ego trying to make sense of it all. Eventually when she sees her overreaction, she is forced to take a long hard look at herself, and her ability to trust the man she loves and the friend she cherishes.

AFTERWORD

by

Douglas G. Clarke

* * *

WATER

Douglas Adams had a knack for giving inanimate objects human characteristics. In one of his stories, he described the fog creeping down an alleyway. This image has stayed with me for many years. In a nod to him, I decided to write in this style about water. As I wrote, the water morphed from an inanimate object with human characteristics into a living, thinking creature.

In these mirky waters of the swamp, I see reflections of my own life by the way the water had to find strength within itself to hold onto its dream, while those around it gave up and died. Another reflection is when the water had to realize that sometimes pain is required in order to succeed.

CARBON NEUTRAL

What I was trying to show in the story is the thought process behind the decisions we make in life. For Jill and John the choice was between the comforts of life and the need to have a child.

I didn't start out writing a tragedy, but as the story progressed I found that the central question was really answered on the first day. For them a child was more important. Because of that, the point of the story became, "Was that the right choice?" To answer that question I needed to tell their life story. To do that in so few words, I had their lives last only three more days.

Siting on their porch waiting for the world to end, Jill and John could look back at their decision and know for sure that the experience of starting a family was infinitely more satisfying than having a new car and a new job.

***

CHASING REFLECTIONS

In this story I wanted to parallel Chris's struggle through the maze of mirrors and her social struggle of getting the boy she desired. The maze has mirrors, dead-ends, invisible barriers, and shifting walls, but it also has unexpected help along the way.

The mirrors show reflections of reality. In the maze the reflections show Chris's distorted view of herself, where she is going, and Julie. In real life mirrors are how we see ourselves reflected in other people. For Chris, Julie reflected a low self-esteem of being a stupid loser.

The maze's dead-end parallels the pointlessness of asking and demanding that Julie must give back the ticket. A larger point of senselessness is trying to win a boy's heart by buying a kiss from him. Both Chris and Julie are trapped by this misconception of believing that if Julie kisses him first, then he won't ever look at Chris.

The panes of glass that block the way in the maze reflect both the physical barriers in our lives, like the distance from the exit of the maze to the kissing booth that can't be covered in time, and emotional barriers, that keep us from reaching our goals.

Moving walls are often the most frustrating part of life. Whether it is a dropped ticket that throws well-laid plans into chaos, someone else wining the race, getting lost, the process of starting over, or of re-evaluating where you are and where you want to go, these can be emotional and spiritually disturbing events. But rules do change, and adapting to these changes is what life is about

Unexpected help can come in many forms, from someone reaching out to meet a need they see to the realization that the reflections you are seeing are distorted. In this story, all of Chris's misconceptions of herself and how others viewed her came crashing down when she found out that all the boys wanted to kiss her, and not Julie.

In the end, the difference between Chris and Julie is shown. Julie was more excited about one-upping Chris and proving she was better, while Chris didn't even notice Julie because her focus was on Robert.

*A*FTERWORD

by

Laura Stafford

* * *

MAPLE LEAF RAG

In very short stories, especially flash fiction such as this, it is difficult to include an element of backstory or flashbacks. It takes too many words to explain what happened in the before, and how it affects the now and after. So to use this literary device effectively, each word must be considered carefully, to provide clarity without bogging down the plot or slowing the action of the story.

With *Maple Leaf Rag*, it was my intention to experiment including this backstory to give the reader a portrait of a community man who has a past deeper than we can imagine. It is this subtle backstory that gives *Maple Leaf Rag* its twisted ending and allows the reader to recognize the true nature of the lead character.

TALKING TURKEY

This story is one of my favorites because it depicts a typical holiday family dinner in my house. Opinions and debates dominate the conversation, sometimes leading to heated, shouting arguments.

But the joy of these dinners, especially for me as a writer, is that they give me insight into how other people think. We can never agree - we're always pushing each's others views and beliefs, testing the knowledge and convictions of one another - and it makes for awkward, yet interesting holidays.

Talking Turkey explores the ways that a strong family can question each other, debate, argue, even fight, and still find love and affection for each other despite disagreements.

* * *

RUTH-LESS

I'm intrigued by disappearances - they pique the feelings of horror and fear of the unknown; knowing that the missing person has most likely succumbed to some unimaginable fate.

But what about those people who just seem to

vanish into thin air - right before your eyes? *Ruth-Less* explores the possibility that someone can fade away on the wind, in a moment of confusion, never to be heard from again, all in an instant and without warning.

Would there be someone to blame? Would you blame someone even if there was no one to accuse?

* * *

MEET THE GIRLFRIEND

My father has always taught me that you should take each person as they come, judge them for who they are and what qualities they choose to represent themselves with. We have all been stereotyped, grouped with others despite our individuality. When we think of prejudice, we usually talk about other races, cultures, religions, but each person's unique being deserves consideration, especially by those closest to us.

As one of the first flash fiction stories I've ever written, I was nervous writing *Meet the Girlfriend* because I didn't think I could tell a story with so few words, so I chose a topic I knew a bit about - prejudice and misconceptions.

Can we ever really know someone?

$\mathcal{A}$FTERWORD

by

Kristen Strassel

* * *

RIDING OUT THE STORM

Independence Day is the quintessential American holiday. The official kickoff of summer. So what if it snowed that day? Then we'd know that climate change was really here. What would that mean for our planet if our seasons flipped and twisted so we could never take anything for granted? What else would we not be able to take for granted anymore?

To stay true to tradition, this is where I've watched the Fourth of July parade for ages. Of course, no one has ever blown up the plaza, but it's never snowed on the Fourth either—yet.

*** *

NIGHTSHADE PARK

I have a thing for vampires. Other supernatural creatures just don't do it for me. Vampires live forever and break all the rules—and look super hot doing it. I consider vampire stories modern fairy tales, and my full-length novel is a vampire book. This was the only one of the short stories I managed to incorporate into a vampire tale.

I also love amusement parks. I don't care how old I get, I never will outgrow craving the thrill of the roller coaster. It's just such a simple pleasure that can make anyone forget all their worries for a few minutes.

The combination of the two seemed like the perfect marriage of thrill seeking, so I couldn't resist writing about them when the opportunity presented itself.

*** *

THE REUNION

One thing I always knew for sure is that I had no plans of going to any of my high school reunions. I hardly had any interest in being in high school when I was enrolled. If I wanted to keep in touch with those people, I would have. I still am in touch with many of my high school friends. If you weren't my friend, I simply don't care.

As Facebook grew in popularity, all those high school people came out of the woodwork. I added them. Hey, why not? Guess what? I lost interest. Even worse were the people from my private elementary school who tried to *friend* me on Facebook. They certainly didn't try to *friend* me in school. No, thank you. I guess that fancy education didn't do anything to improve their memory.

What is the moral? Surround yourself with interesting people who make your life better. Let all those boring leeches wonder what happened to you.

* * *

POSTCARDS FROM PARADISE

I've always been afraid of flying. I guess it's a control thing. I used to scare the other passengers when all the blood drained from my face, and I clung to my chair for dear life. I'm way better now, although I'm still extremely religious during take off.

Flying over water still scares me, and I have yet to do it. This is stupid, I know. A plane crash is a plane crash. No matter what you fall down on, you remain pretty much in the *screwed* category.

What's the worst that can happen? I always think of George Carlin's famous bit about airplane safety. I don't ever want to be floating through the ocean clinging to a pillow full of beer farts. But that makes for a boring story unless George is telling it. What if the plane crashed on a island that civilization had yet to touch? Enter *Postcards from Paradise.* Chances are, this island probably doesn't have mail delivery.

This summer I will be going to Europe for the first time. I will be flying over water for the first time. I will try to keep it together.

$\mathcal{A}$FTERWORD

by

Jot Russell

* * *

BAITING HOLLOW

Many a scary story has been told around campfires within the dark woods of Baiting Hollow Scout Camp. I should know, because I was one of those scouts. Over the years altered variations of stories have been passed down about the landmarks that somehow retain their names: Owl's Curse, Suicide Hill, Shipwreck Cove and, of course, Fishman Swamp. If you find yourself walking the north shore beaches of Long Island and happen across high tide's flow into a dark marshy thicket, think twice before you enter. *He's waiting...*

***

BAD RAIN

When I was in South Pacific once on business, there was a storm that rained down several inches an hour until all the low-lying streets and cellars were flooded. The locals called this a *bad rain* and acted as if it was a normal occurrence. When the waters receded, mud that had run down the vertical slopes created a thick layer that covered the roads and sidewalks. Within hours the united people set their shovels and brooms to work until the city was back in business— resuscitated from the choking effects of Mother Nature's wrath. If we all work together, even the seemingly insurmountable task of solving climate change is within our reach. Extend a hand.

HALLOWEEN RITUAL

A distant relative recently found me through Ancestry.com. My mother, Joan Russell, was amazed by the history he had collected of the family she had lost at such a young age. When she was six, and just a month after the infamous attack on Pearl Harbor, her father was one of forty-eight soles lost to sea aboard the naval submarine, S-26. My grandfather's resemblance carries on within the faces of my brother and me. Little did I know how far back genes retain their influence. You see, my newly discovered third cousin provided me a picture of my grandfather's grandfather, and it looked just like my brother Phil. The story of this man was not one of peace and sanity, as his crazy nature led him to be institutionalized. I know now where my brother gets his crazy nature.

My temporary profile picture was once my great-great-grandfather, William Lawrence Russell, who died in Maryland's National Hospital for the Insane back in October of 1900.

***

FIRE ISLAND

Divorce has taught me about the painful misunderstandings that normally exist between a husband and wife. But instead of taking a chance to reveal the hidden negative perceptions that collect like bricks in a wall between, many seek a fresh start with one they have yet to form those bricks with. How better to uncover the mask they shroud themselves behind, than to paint a picture through their eyes?

AFTERWORD

by

Richard Bunning

* * *

RIBBIT-RIBBIT

HELP RUN

FROGS-FROGS

Life tends to be *nasty, brutish, and short.* This is particularly true if one happens to be a frog. Most frogs have so many enemies, from lizards and snakes, through cats and birds, to man. It has been a long time since the reptiles of the Earth were in control of things. The dinosaurs had a good run at being boss creatures—before they got bashed up by a meteorite, or was it a vast Vogon space cruiser, or something else entirely? But that was all 66 million years ago. The frogs as a collective body, the huge *Order of Anura*, must think it is high time they gained military dominion over the Earth.

I don't know whether the frogs have read Hobbes's

Levianthan, but they must at times consider the idea of imposing their *Order* on what they surly must see as the savage chaos of mankind. Certainly most Human activities have proved to be disastrous for the Anura, so who of us could blame them for wanting to get their own back? Frogs need marshes, estuaries, wet forests, and all the nutritious bugs and insects that man is so keen to eradicate. And what is it mankind does the most, if not turn the wetlands into deserts, and bury the deserts under impenetrable layers of reconstituted rock? Man is literally cutting the foundations, the vital pillars, the very legs from under the Anurian world.

***

THE AL GORE RHYTHM

OF

CLIMATE CHANGE

The debate about climate change, or perhaps we should say shifting climate patterns, is going to ebb and flow for well, possibly ever. In reality the debate cannot end, became even when the macro, the climate, is going through a fairly stable period, the micro, the weather, can still bobble about like a particularly unstable yo-yo.

Heralding as I do, from the British Isles I'm particularly aware of weather. British people sometimes talk about little else. We even greet each other with tidbits of usually obvious weather news: *Good day, It's a bit nippy out*, or *It's raining cats and dogs, It never rains but it pours, I've forgotten what the sun looks like, I hate these dark wet mornings*, or if you want a long chat then, *Do you remember the year when we had a summer?* The answer to the last comment will probably contain one of the rare years— 1911, 1955, 1976 or 2011—depending on where in the Isles you live and how old you are.

As someone from a relatively cold miserable part of the planet, it is actually quite hard not to be secretly pleased that there may be a trend to warmer times. One's view might very much reflect whether one likes the weather warmer or not, or whether one wishes it was wetter or not, and from which direction the wind will come next.

I'd rather sport a parasol than an umbrella, but which do you prefer to carry?

THE IMPENDING DEATH

OF

HARLEQUIN

Based on the song, *The Carnival is Over* by The
Seekers (1965), words by Tom Springfield.

The song, *The Carnival is Over*, made quite an impact
on my then young mind. I remember my family having
often played a 45 single of it. The voice of Judith
Durham became a part of my stronger childhood
memories. The words meant very little back then, but
her voice and the haunting melody have become part of
who I am. I'm sure different music and different voices
do the same for us all. They work as anchors on our
memories, our personal anthems. As an adult I slowly
started to make sense of the words, which have now
given me this story.

Usually I see flash fiction as an episode in a longer
story, though this was an exception. The 750 words
proved just enough, leaving me with no desire to take
the story further. That isn't to say that potential for story
development is lacking, not a bit of it. Usually I'm
struggling to keep a story's integrity whilst reducing the
words.

***

FIRST VENICE,
SOON LONDON

This story was written in the light of the Costa Concordia disaster and against a background of growing popularity of cruises. Unbelievably, one of the details that came out of the Concordia tragedy was that the company couldn't reconcile the apparent number of crew with their records. I can find no legal evidence that this issue has ever been resolved. I am aware that a considerable number of Filipinos worked on this cruise liner, being amongst the population groups that are most often employed in the industry. It is common knowledge that the working days are very long, run unbroken for months and months at a time, and support very little leave in between.

I hope that my use of local language is accurate enough to not cause offence. I would be grateful to hear from readers if correction is necessary. I must make it clear that I am fortunate indeed to have been on a Costa Cruise. That voyage made for one of the best holidays I have ever had. The crew was fantastically polite and hard working. I find it impossible to believe that the company's crew and customer manifests aren't now as accurate as aircraft ones have to be.

As for migration, legal or not, if I was in poor circumstance and was brave enough to better my life by migration, I might. Equally, no nation could then be blamed for using any reasonable force to stop me. It is difficult to judge the rights or wrongs of migration unless one has been on both sides of the fence.

$\mathcal{A}$FTERWORD

by

Alli Vaughan

* * *

AIZAWA TAVERN

When people think of swamps, they tend to think of the bayou in the US. Here we have a swamp in a very different setting, in Japan, a country associated with mystic beauty and intrigue. It is not a place you would expect to find backwood folks. I like the idea of blending unexpected scenarios with unlikely heroes and villains. In this story the snake man is a deadly predator, and the protagonist has fallen into his den.

***

SYSA'S STAR

The race is on, and I love a good action story. Why not weave in an elf and a sorcerer to boot? Sysa is the innocent apprentice of a great wizard, one with great power. Because of her humble nature and possibly her stature, the wizard had overlooked just how powerful she was. But when Sysa is put to the test, she saves her master and the fate of her world.

***

BAKE AND THE PREDATOR

Poor Bake. The price of compliance can often be more then you bargained for. In the beginning of the story, mirrors serve as a tool to show how fragmented he is and foretell his distortion of the future. His fate is sealed when he walks into the fun house. He loves Shelia and knows just how extreme her greed has become. Instead of dealing with that, he sweeps the problem under a rug, like many people do in their own relationships.

WEDDING MASKS

My style tends toward the fantastic and the mystical. For me the challenge lies in writing something that can happen in modern day. In *Wedding Masks,* I took what I consider a plausible plot in the muggle world and added elements that I love to sprinkle into fantasy—the unsure damsel, the gallant hero, a slew of awful guests to serve as antagonists. In this story the protagonist is able to awaken to a flaw that has kept her stunted.

$\mathscr{A}$FTERWORD

by

Harry Alexiou

* * *

ENSLAVED - 1831

This was an interesting and educational story for me to write. I originally wanted to be factual about swamp life and centre my story on the realities of its ecosystem. However, once I'd started to delve into the plethora of web pages thrown up by my broad search, I realised that there was a lot of history that encompassed swamp life and the slave trade of the nineteenth century in the United States. I pawed over pages and pages of interesting articles that discussed the flora and fauna of the swamps. The articles that really drew my attention were the ones that discussed the treatment of the African Americans during the harsh epoch of slavery and the suffering that resulted. My story is just a glimpse into the physical and mental pain and the despair suffered by those who were separated from family and quite often sold off as commodities to the highest bidders. The ending, for me and hopefully for you, allowed for a glimmer of hope in the great dismal swamp.

* * *

NATURE AND THE GIANTS

This short tale of the energy industry and the benefits of renewable energy was stimulated by the constant news reports surrounding the greenhouse effect. Apparently our planet is being strangled by carbon emissions and all manner of pollutants. World weather patterns are noticeably extreme in recent years and the finger points at the industrial world and the burning of fossil fuels. There are those who argue that the whole greenhouse effect discussion is just a smoke screen (no pun intended) for the opportunity for governments to boost coffers via *carbon emission* taxes. What is the reason for all the weather disruption in recent years? Some experts will put the blame on a decade long period of intense solar storms that are set to peak this year (2013). Ironic really that we are looking to the sun as one possible alternative to fossil fuels, and it is reputedly the sun which is to blame for all the weird weather patterns the world over. The story is thankfully pure fiction, and I do not imply for one second that the big oil and energy companies would go to such destructive lengths to protect their profits and businesses. Perhaps diversification is the key.

* * *

THE KING'S SECRET

The idea that those in a position of power have something to hide is not new. In this case it is rather extreme and disgusting—I have to admit. I tend to shy away from graphic scenes of blood and gore, so there are no details regarding entrails or detailed dismembering. There are many writers who specialise in the art and do a very good job—if that's your cup of tea. I would rather leave it to them for now. I quite liked the idea of Joel not realising Ursula's feelings for him whilst he continued to be smitten with Miranda. His last chance to tell Miranda how he felt had been cut short and remained unspoken. Did Joel escape? Would he have ended up in the arms of Ursula if he did? Maybe.

GUARDIAN OF THE LAKE

Guardian of the Lake is a fantasy story of a race of peaceful people. They are a new generation deciding that they want more, not happy with their lot. The grass is possibly greener on the other side, and the Vorkans will go to war to satisfy this burning desire. Their leader is swayed by their desire and like a president wanting votes it could be a winner. The Vorkans would not be dissimilar to any invading force in the modern world. The mask is easily a symbol of the mask we all wear or one that the governments of the world show us. The mask can keep us safe, can open doors, and help us get ahead, or make us fit in better to a crowd. We all have our own masks, but nobody can be like anybody else. The mask must fit—your mask. The hesitation of young Shardan to tell his father the truth is indicative of the dilemma faced by many young people in modern life. "What will dad say?" Instead, the boy chooses to hide the truth. Even though this could be fatal for the campaign and all of his people, he would rather let it be and save himself from being branded a coward and likely executed. Self preservation.

$\mathcal{A}$FTERWORD

by

Oliver Dolan

* * *

OLD ELLERBE

When writing *Old Ellerbe*, I tried to imagine what it would be like to be a lonely and ashamed middle-aged man, reeling from a nasty divorce and the loss of custody of his only child. I knew that if I were in those shoes, I'd want to run away to a place where I felt comfortable, preferably one where I spent time as a child. The main character, Italo, returns to his great grandfather's swamp-side cottage, and he learns of Old Ellerbe's existence through a newly formed friendship—something that can be very therapeutic after a tragic life event. Little did Italo know that he was also becoming friends with a large reptile who'd been living on the Indigo Estate for many years.

There are times in our lives where we seek revenge for something someone did to us, and although we may feel bad about seeking it, we seek it nonetheless. In this case Old Ellerbe comes through for Italo, helps him get revenge, and permanently reunites with his son.

***

TIME CAPSULE

I wrote this story right around the time when Hurricane Sandy was pummeling the East Coast with incredible amounts of rain and wind. I took a walk to the corner store one night—halfway through writing—and was thinking to myself, *What if this is the beginning of the end of the world?* I kind of took that idea and ran with it, and was fascinated with the notion that maybe someone, a long time ago, could have predicted an eventual end to our planet caused by our own recklessness and disregard. In *Time Capsule*, the main character's childhood discovery puts him on a lifelong mission to help foster a cleaner, healthier, and a more sustainable planet.

* * *

MY TERRIBLE TUX

My Terrible Tux is a story of a college romance gone bad—really bad. When writing the story, I thought about what it would be like to own a profitable expanding business with someone special, but the relationship was deteriorating. As the business got better and better, the romantic aspect got worse and worse. I focused on the greed of Joyce and the hopefulness of Scott, and I decided that a beach trip to meet the girl's *parents* would be the perfect theme for the story. People aren't always who they seem to be or who they say they are, and this story displays a classic, yet terrifying case of deception.

THE BEACH BUNKER

The Beach Bunker was the first short story I ever put together. When writing the story, I was at a time in my life where I just wanted to hit the pause button, collect myself, and return when I was ready. I dreamt up a scenario where the main character could—after making it through many obstacles—make a conscious decision to take a break from life and collect his thoughts. In my mind the best place to take a break is at the beach: calming waves, soft sand, and a beaming sun have a way of relaxing the soul. I think *The Beach Bunker* shows us that it is important to take chances, and always remember that even though we can't take a break from life, we can still seek out a place where we're at peace— one where we can relax, be ourselves, and refuel for future adventures.

$\mathcal{A}$FTERWORD

by

H. M. Schuldt

❊ ❊ ❊

TESSA ROSEWOOD
& THE GREEN RIVER

When I sat down to write a story that takes place in a swamp, I thought about all the real people in life who go missing. Some are found, but some are not. I asked myself, "What would happen if a sixteen-year old girl went missing in a little swamp town?" In this story, not only does Tessa's high school friend go missing in Green River, Louisiana, but Tessa also loses her cell phone. Quite often in real life when a disaster strikes, another problem is just around the corner. I tried to show how Tessa would not give up her search no matter what. She would stick with it until she found her friend, all the while hoping that she would find her friend alive.

In *Tessa Rosewood & The Green River*, Tessa's best friend, Valerie, disappears. I wanted to show how various people react to such a frightening incident. This story is filled with suspense, and it is very realistic. Who could be responsible for Valerie's disappearance? Is it her boyfriend, Victor? Is it crazy Milton's dad? Did Valerie run away? Find out what happened to Valerie when you read *Tessa Rosewood & The Green River*.

* * *

TORNADO PAPARAZZI

After hearing about several devastating deaths of those who chase tornadoes, I decided to write a short story about fictional emergency responders called Windmen who know how to quickly locate houses in harm's way and are equipped to rescue those who are stuck inside. In my story, *Tornado Paparazzi*, I wanted to show the difference between those who chase after tornadoes for the fun of it and those who set out to rescue citizens in danger. Some of the storm chasers who chase after tornadoes do so for a thrill and to possibly sell photos. Many of these storm chasers have died in attempt to take pictures up close. Some of these storm chasers are able to identify the speed of a twister, the size of it, and the distance it travels. Wouldn't it be great to train emergency responders and quip them with the knowledge of how to rescue citizens who might be stuck in a house? Wouldn't it be better to develop equipment that can quickly identify people in harms way? For a long time, we've had firemen who can rescue people who are stuck in a building on fire. It's time we train Windmen and develop better equipment that can provide critical information to save lives. In *Tornado Paparazzi*, a family must leave home or risk staying in their house while a tornado passes over.

***

CANDY CARNIVAL

I've always been intrigued by carnival characters and carnival acts. Before writing this story I asked myself several questions. *What kind of person would try to manage a carnival? What kind of person would sign up to work in a carnival? What goes on behind the scenes at a carnival?* In my story, the owner and manager, Fireball Deborah, has a good head for business and for finding carnival talent. It's no secret that carnivals need enough money to stay in business, and some of the carnivals provide questionable games where patrons are unable to win. Fireball Deborah has found a way to make her carnival successful with people like Brooks and his sister, Candy.

Fireball Deborah finds Brooks, an accurate knife thrower, and presents him as the main act because of his talent and charm. I wanted to show a contrast between Brooks and his sister, Candy, by having Candy at the carnival with different skills and a completely different personality. Even though Brooks and Candy come from a wealthy family and they both have good looks, one sibling is a good talker while the other one isn't. Brooks has the unusual skill of throwing knives and can impress a crowd with the handsome way he carries himself, while Candy is better at communicating in person and getting her way. Candy's big problem is that she has not learned how to be a content person in life. She's always living on the edge, looking for the next big thrill. Underneath it all, Brooks and Candy both have a mother who wholeheartedly disapproves of the strange lifestyle of being a carnival worker.

* * *

LAGO LANDER ON MARS

What is better than searching for life on Mars? Some think it is to figure out a way to *start* life on Mars. When writing this story, I researched various projects in regards to life on Mars. I found out that there are multiple goals for each Mars mission. As a writer, I began to use my imagination by asking questions. *What would happen if the atmosphere could be stabilized in one area on Mars? What if machines were sent to Mars, farming machines that could plant seeds in the summer?*

Tungsten, the main character in my story, is a woman who operates one of nine spaceships from Earth. Once on Mars, she sends out a flying scope to locate Curiosity, while waiting for the other spaceships to land.

Previously, Curiosity had discovered a strange pot down in a cave, but was unable to reach inside this mysterious man-made item. Tungsten's scope is supposed to find out what is hidden inside this unusual pot. *How did the pot arrive on Mars?* I suddenly began to think about the backstory.

In this story, *Lago Lander On Mars*, readers will see life on Mars—plant material and selective animals—and possibly find much, much more.

$\mathcal{A}$FTERWORD

by

Randy Dutton

* * *

THE SWAMP TRADER

This is one of the first times I've written a nontechnical fantasy story. It was fun. I extended the timeline of a story that depicts hallucinogenic fungus, a tainted food affecting Van Gogh's painting style to the distant future. Weapons have reverted to the most basic technology and the environment has changed and is propelling society's collapse. While some cling to a modicum of control, barbarism will ever be attempting to crush civilization.

THE PHYTOPLANKTON
CARBON TRAP

I'm a technology junkie who likes incorporating real science into my work. My story relates to, but was not included, in my first novel, *The Carbon Trap*, an ecopolitical thriller, whereby mankind uses genetically modified life-forms to decrease global carbon dioxide. Phytoplankton means 'wandering plant' and is responsible for half of CO_2 absorption by nature, and this story, tries to depict scientists doing things that endanger humanity. I believe this threat is a real possibility and, like Michael Crichton does with his works, want to bring such issues to the fore.

***

OBSESSION

The question posed in this story was asked to my high school graduating class and my best friend gave Omar Khayyam's response and publicly named the classmate of his desire. When the school paper published it, he was ridiculed by many. The popular girl he identified, and whom did not share his affection, was

313

greatly embarrassed. The 'what if' scenario where the nerd manipulates events periodically came to mind, and thus story was born. This is a story that has long legs, and I might turn it into a novel.

* * *

AFTER THE WAVES

Survival after a tsunami is personal. I live near an area that suffers from the type of megathrust tsunami described in my story, roughly every 500 years. The last was in 1700. I set my story in a real town 30 miles from my 124-acre bluff top property. Buying land 205 feet above sea level was intentional. When I ran for the state legislature in 2008, I discovered how unprepared our area and community are and strove to increase planning. This story is part of that awareness.

$\mathcal{A}$FTERWORD

by

Gail Harkins

* * *

EVANGELINE

Perhaps because I wrote Evangeline during the long dark nights of December, I couldn't get the thought of glowing alligators out of my mind! The University of Guelph, Ontario developed glowing pigs for medical research several years ago, and glowing zebra fish are relatively common in laboratories, so why not create a fictional, glowing alligator? I don't know that a glowing alligator is practical, but it was a whimsical and scientifically possible addition to a swamp story.

Admittedly, like my character of Jaimie, I yearn for glowing flora. In my case, the object of my desire is a moonlight garden powered by luciferase. Imagine gardenias glowing softly in the garden... I suspect I have a long wait before I see that reality. Scientists are bent on more practical matters.

***

PETEY AND PAUL

Petey and Paul is the very first short story I ever wrote, although I had written longer works. My husband told me about the short story challenge, and that it involved climate change. My initial response was, "I can't do that! That's not what I write about!" Yet, I continued to mull over the notion. When I remembered a news report about the polar bear census around Churchill, I had my idea. Polar bears are beautiful, majestic, and even comical, but they also are skilled hunters that are, rightly, feared by those who encounter them in the wild. I suspect many people see their beauty and forget the power behind their perceived cuddliness. Paul realized that a bit late.

Some people have speculated about my choice of character names. There is a certain parallel, I suppose, between St. Paul's epiphany on the road to Damascus and Paul's realization about polar bears. That was a subconscious decision, if anything at that level can be called a decision. Consciously, the combination of names merely had a good ring.

***

THE CIRCUS

Writing this story was far more difficult than it should have been. Circuses and amusement parks are fun frivolous places, and I couldn't imagine a story of any sort—much less one that also included an insect and something borrowed or stolen. Perhaps I had cotton candy in my brain. I toyed with a few ideas and discarded them as utter drivel. Finally after far too long, I settled on this story. It may be drivel, too. Sigh. I hope not.

It was inspired by two things, really—a 1910 children's book called *The Circus Boys in Dixie Land – Winning the Plaudits of the Sunny South* and the Beatles' song, *She's Leaving Home*. I decided to flip the stereotypical image of leaving home to join the circus. So, if a circus child left the circus, what would be the attraction? I decided stability, gained through college and an accounting degree, would be a good solution for my character, Ella.

***

THE GOOD HUMOR MAN

Coming home from a local art festival, my husband and I stopped at a Mexican restaurant for an early dinner. Over enchiladas, we discussed Japan's tsunami and the debris field moving westward across the Pacific. A floating dock and a boat that survived Japan's devastating tsunami had recently reached the shores of Oregon and Washington. The news footage was still vivid in our minds. We wondered whether it was possible for anyone to have survived, and whether anyone had been rescued at sea. That gave rise to much speculation regarding what conditions they would face if survival was even possible. Rather than craft a dark story of loss and devastation, I wanted to write a light-hearted survival story ... a gentle romance between two unlikely people who were at the wrong place at the wrong time.

$\mathcal{A}$FTERWORD

by

Sylvia Stein

***

THE MYSTICAL SWAMP

I wrote *The Mystical Swamp*, a story about second chances and the powers of a beautiful creature. Dr. Levitan is a man running from his dark past. He discovers a more powerful message while hiding out in the Louisiana Bayou in the little town of St. Claire.

***

MAD ABOUT SCIENCE

I wrote *Mad about Science* by telling the story of Dr. Edward Monroe whom is a very talented and skilled scientist from Baltimore Maryland. He is contacted by the CDC when there is a contaminant threatening human kind. It is a race against time, and it is up to Dr.

Monroe to try and find the answer.

***

THE LOST TREASURE

I wrote *The Lost Treasure*, a story that I set in London in the 1800's. It is about a young detective by the name of Sebastian Cromwell who is set on finding his deceased father's treasure while accompanied by his two associates. This is a story of a son trying to take back what the British government took from his own father, James.

***

THE ENGAGEMENT PARTY

This story is about trying to keep someone from the past a secret from those around, fearing it might affect new relationships in life. In *The Engagement Party*, this cover up is the case for a young engaged couple. An unexpected person from the past intrudes the party when the young happy couple is celebrating.

$\mathcal{A}$FTERWORD

by

Lynette White

***

PRODIGAL SON

What do you do when someone you loved and respected suddenly disappears? How do you cope when you learn the terrible truth about why they felt they had to leave you behind? Do you keep a promise you made to the one who lied to you? Do you turn your back on the one who needs you the most because you owe them nothing—after all they abandoned you?

Though this story is completely fictional the situation is very real to many people. This story is but a moment in the lives of these two brothers, but I hope the untold story touches every person who shares that moment with Laitin and Asa.

EXODUS

"Their problem is not my problem, and there is no reason to make it my problem." We have all faced this dilemma.

Exodus was the first story I wrote for this series of anthologies and, starting with this story, I decided I would write it in a way that kept the reader pondering for a bit. *Exodus* finds a free spirited wanderer in a situation where he can spare many lives or walk away— after all it isn't his problem.

Do you find yourself walking away, trying to convince yourself it is not your problem? Or do you do what you know is the right thing to do?

* * *

JAROB

"I wish I could remember what that was." How many times have we all said that? Memories seem to be one of those things we are constantly at war with. Some we wish we could remember. Others we wish we could forever banish.

Then there are those who have been robbed of every memory they cherished. Some people suffer from a cruel disease called Alzheimer's. But others simply misplace a memory in the wonderful file cabinet we call a brain. I wish we all had our own Jarob.

I also want to take a moment to recognize the millions of people who remain nameless for many different reasons. May they never be forgotten.

* * *

HOMECOMING

Jilted love is the one thing every human being seems to experience at some point. There is a moment when your whole world collapses, and you feel like you can't take another breath.

Most people slowly recover, and somehow the world rights itself again, but what if you know that person was the one you were meant for? What if they come crawling back and beg for a second chance? Were there tears of joy or tears from a broken heart that would never forgive? You finish Brit and Derrick's story.

$\mathcal{A}$FTERWORD

by

Janet Bond

✳ ✳ ✳

SWAMP ISLAND

In *Swamp Island* two friends travel to see if a legend is true, the legend of mermaids. When they arrive at the island, it is full of different trees—something you don't see too much of. They walk until they reach a muddy looking swamp. I want my readers to find out how two friends find mermaids. But the friends didn't know that the mermaids want them—as a meal. The friends accept that the mermaids went into their room without coming out. Even in times of trouble, the friends never left each other's side.

*** *

THE OLD SCHOOL

The old school is about a brother and sister doing something their mother told them not to do. In *The Old School*, Jan and Jessie explore a haunted school to see if it is really haunted. Because if their disobedience, their mother makes them go back to the school to teach them a lesson. She wants them to know, "Don't go lookin' for somethin'. You just might find it. If the ghosts ain't messin' with you, you don't go messin' with them."

*** *

TUNNEL OF DOOM

I wrote the *Tunnel of Doom* to show two friends, Tony and Jessie, who even though they grew up together, Tony let envy get in the way of their friendship. Jessie asks Tony, "Do you want to go on a trip with me to the carnival?" Tony says yes and brings two friends along with them. After being at the carnival for a while, they go into the Tunnel of Doom. Tony and her friends set it up to scare Jessie. Jessie loses her trust in Tony because Jessie thought something bad had happened to Tony. Tony and her friends laugh at Jessie. Jessie gets very upset and hurt by Tony. Tony tries to apologize to Jessie, but Jessie loses all her trust in Tony. It reminds me of life today—the ones you are close to can betray you.

* * *

BOCA GRANDE KEY

Boca Grande Key is about Cami and her brother Kaleb spending time together by going on a trip. They end up on Boca Grande Key because the boat was being pulled by some kind of a force. Cami sees a strange looking man who is a ghost. The ghost wants them to follow him into the water. Kaleb gets caught in the water, and the ghost man shows Kaleb a boat as well as several human skeletons. Kaleb is about to sink when his sister pulls him out. The ghost man and other people were previously killed on the island. I want my readers to know why the island was haunted.

*A*FTERWORD

by

Colleen Sayre

* * *

BUBBA

What really goes on in a deep dark swamp? As humans we think we have the upper hand, but late at night when the creepy crawlies slither out from the muck and the mud, another world exists. Growing up in the south where every mud puddle, no matter how small, usually has at least one gator living in it, I gained a healthy respect for nature's hierarchy. *Bubba* is a peek into the swampy edges of my mind—and my world.

AFTERWORD

by

Scott Amis

***

GATOR CHOW

In concept and setting, *Gator Chow* is atmospheric, dark, and questioning. Two best war buddies working on government contract are sent to track and apprehend a dangerous criminal hiding deep in a swamp, but family ties and the promise of quick wealth compromise the deep friendship and loyalty that can only come on shared battlefields. The heretofore honorable veteran Harold makes a fast and deadly decision that will make him a rich man, but what will his life hold from this day onward?

***

BUT A VIKING'S TALE

A knight, Thierré de Coudre, his younger brother and understudy, Galien, and their father Henri are principal characters in *To Shine With Honor*, my work-in-progress trilogy. It tells the story of a French family of minor nobility and their trials and adventures before, during, and after the First Crusade (1086–1118).

In developing the concept for *But a Viking's Tale,* I found an interesting and fun opportunity to introduce an element of superstitious folktale. It came to life in a previously developed fictional setting based on historical fact with Thierré and Galien de Coudre, re-invented as medieval zombie hunters. The themes of knightly courage and honor, a close family, and a strong bond between brothers are present in *To Shine With Honor* and are fundamental elements in *But a Viking's Tale.*

$\mathcal{A}$FTERWORD

by

Andy Lake

* * *

RISING

FROM THE WATERS

Just a few miles from where I live, the Fens in East Anglia are the desolate setting for this historical sub-Gothic tale of loss and love. The narrator is a father telling his son about an earlier time, of darkness and disorder, around 600 years before. His tale is set just after the Norman conquest of England and the revolt of Hereward the Wake. In the narrator's time, at the Restoration after the reign of Oliver Cromwell, the low-lying swamps and marshland of the Fens have recently been drained. Despite the recent traumas of the Civil War, this is a wealthier and more orderly world the narrator is living in.

He tells a story of two desperate people brought together through their loss and the exhaustion of grief and despair. From the narrator's point of view, it is about overcoming terrors—whether demonic or stemming from the wickedness of men—through the power of love. His own and his son's existence are living proof of this power.

$\mathcal{A}$FTERWORD

by

Jenise Erikson

* * *

SWAMP CYCLES

Swamp Cycles actualized from my childhood raised in a cabinet shop, my life as a Louisiana native, and the economic downturn in recent years affecting our state. When the economy threatens the livelihood of those living off the land in the swamps of French speaking south Louisiana, families feel they must adapt and modify to new circumstances to survive, perhaps going beyond acceptable community avenues for subsistence. Family businesses are often passed on from one generation to the next, and agreements aren't always unanimous. Dependent upon their environment's provisions, families find ways to perpetuate trade, to sustain the family business, and to appease both the investors and clients. It is sometimes a delicate balancing act. Lisette adjusts and refines her decisions to preserve her family's livelihood. Desperate circumstances breed extreme measures for anyone struggling to survive, whether they live in the urban city streets, rural suburbia, or the isolated depths of the timeless wetlands.

AFTERWORD

by

Mike Boggia

* * *

FREEDOM FLIGHT

Inspiration came from a picture of a sad child crossing a bridge leading to a dismal forest. It brought back memories of childhood, bullying, and the urge to flee cruelty. A forest and a swamp on the property where I grew up were a refuge and fodder for the stories I began to write as a kid. At one time or another we all want to find a safe place where we are accepted and loved.

For more information about

Giant Tales Books,

please visit:

writers750.com